GATHERING DARK

VITUS SWINGGATE BOOK ONE

DANIEL KLAPHEKE

PROLOGUE

The corpse lay in the leaf litter, thawing beside the campfire. The dancing flames illuminated his face and glinted off the brass buckles on his uniform. His gray skin pulled tight over his eye sockets and sharp cheek bones. The yellow bone of his forehead showed where skin had peeled away during his exhumation. His blue fingers were twisted and gnarled. One hand curled into a loose fist as if clutching uselessly to the living world. His eyes, glassy and fogged over, stared lifelessly at the dark branches swaying overhead, oblivious that the shadowy forest around us teemed with peril.

The dead man had no worries about hordes of savages creeping around in the dark understory, or the witch of the woods watching from the boughs of the trees. He had no fear of predators stalking the campsite, or of phantoms lurking about. He had no concern that his fellow bluebelly Invaders could be closing in on our camp at any moment. He was long dead. His body frozen stiff. In an odd, macabre way, I almost envied him. I had become an abomination. Only thirteen years old and I was spending New Year's Eve in the lonely wilderness of Dead Goat Hollow. Alone. Utterly alone. My only company was the body of a man I had killed months ago.

ONE
SPRING 1861

The game trail I'd been following faded among the dark green stalks of a canebrake just before the westerly road. I pushed toward the roadside, weaving through the riot of segmented shafts. Three figures ambled in the distance, approaching from the west. I recognized their shapes and demeanors. I crawled on the damp forest floor. My haversack, heavy with smelly cargo, bumped along and hung up on the stalks as I negotiated the woody maze. A few yards from the road, I found an opening in the foliage and leveled a stem of devil's walking stick, aiming it like a sniper's rifle. I took three pretend shots before creeping forward again, preparing to ambush the travelers.

I sat on my haunches, waiting. A light wind coursed through the canopy, whistling and gushing through the long, thin cane leaves. The grass-like stems, swaying and dancing, brushed against me, almost knocking me off balance. Hunger gnawed at me. My stomach grumbled as I waited.

Several paces ahead of the others, my best friend Chester kicked a stone as he walked. The stone skipped across the hard-pan dirt, hitting a horseshoe rut, bouncing into the grass. His older brother, George swung a stick back and forth at piles of dried horse dung on the road. My brother, James, sauntered beside George, engaged in a soliloquy, kicking the heads off early buttercups growing in the grass between wagon tracks. George listened intently as James reported on the news he'd heard about a recent attack.

As they neared, I crept closer and sprang forth, roaring like a bear. Chester overreacted and threw himself off the opposite side of the road into a patch of budding briars, upsetting a flock of complaining sparrows. James and George hardly flinched.

"Tarnation, Vitus!" Chester said as he composed himself. "What's wrong with you?"

"Get some paper, I'll start a list," my big brother said. He looked at me with a smile. "Where've you been ole boy?"

"On an expedition," I answered.

"Ma's worried about you."

"Why?"

"You've been gone longer than usual," he said as he slapped my back. "God above! You smell like hell warmed over!"

I sniffed my armpit. He wasn't wrong.

"There's been some developments since you left," James said.

"Developments?"

"Yeah, the Confederates attacked Fort Sumter."

"Isn't that in South Carolina?" I said.

"Yep, that's right."

"What does that mean?" I asked.

"Not sure." He kicked George's heel, trying to trip him.

"Knock it off, fart sniffer!"

"I hope you at least caught something," James said as he kicked me in the pants.

"I did," I said. "Two otters. But it took longer than I thought. Snagged 'em the third day."

"I told Ma you'd be fine."

"Where you all headed, anyway?" I asked.

"Whitton's," George said. "And maybe stir up some trouble in town."

"You comin' along, Vit?" Chester asked.

"Might as well," I said. "Can we swing by Rainey's so I can try and sell these pelts?" I asked James.

"'Spose so."

"But can we avoid the McEwen house?"

Chester chuckled at my request. "Why, cause you smell so bad?"

"Yeah, you afraid a certain someone will find you repulsive?" James teased.

"Well, I have been in the forest for a few days," I defended. "I can't always smell of daisies like you dapper gentlemen."

"Can't make any promises," James said.

"Hey pard, wanna race to Campbell pond?" Chester challenged. Before I could answer, he had started running.

"Why does he even try?" I heard George say as I took off.

I was under the oak tree by Campbell Pond well before Chester. I had grabbed a handful of loblolly pine needles along the way and was rubbing it all over my clothes before he came to a stop, huffing and puffing with his hands on his knees. I crammed another bundle of needles in my mouth.

"I'm getting faster though," Chester said between breaths.

"You sure are, pard."

"Watcha chewin' on there? Doesn't look like you're enjoying it much."

"Loblolly," I garbled. "Just in case we have any interactions in town." The needles smelled like soap, and they tasted awful. I spit it out as James and George approached.

"Chester, why do you even try?" George said. "You've never gotten close to beating Vitus in a foot race. In fact, none of us have."

"Speak for yourself," James said as he gave George a shove. "I can beat this little turd."

"You haven't yet," George reminded him and flashed me a wink.

"Piss off," James retorted.

The four of us continued down the road toward Franklin in self-reflection. I picked a sassafras leaf shaped like a mitten, wadded it up, and stuffed it in my mouth. It was slightly sweet and made me salivate as I chewed it. As we walked along, I pelted the dirt with gobs of spit until I was eventually free of the residual pine taste. As fields turned into lawns on the outskirts of town, James broke the silence. "Do you ever feel like something big is about to happen?" he said to no one in particular. "Like a big event we're destined to be a part of. Something historic."

"Whad a ya mean, pard?" George asked.

"Maybe war. What if this Fort Sumter thing means war? We might have some excitement in our lives."

"We've got plenty of excitement," George countered.

"Not real excitement," said James. "Vitus, what's that quote you told me that day we were hunting sap?" He referred to collecting maple sap in the southern woods of our property. "It was something about desperation. You remember?"

I remembered. We'd collected dozens of buckets of sap back in February. After lugging them a furlong, we boiled it down to a record amount of syrup and candy.

"Yes, it was Henry David Thoreau," I said.

"Well, what was it he said?" James said impatiently.

"The mass of men lead lives of quiet desperation," I quoted.

"Yes, exactly," James said. "That's what I mean, George. Maybe we're leading lives of quiet desperation."

"I don't even know what that means," George said.

James momentarily became lost in thought as he stared at the clouds. "I feel like it's coming."

"What's coming."

"Something big. You know, like maybe right now is the calm before the storm," said James. "I don't know, something just feels weird. Look around. Listen."

Maybe it was only James's influence, but I suddenly felt like something was indeed amiss. Nothing I could put my finger on, but just a feeling.

Mrs. Kelley sat on her front porch in a ladder back chair crocheting. She was usually quick to invite us up for a spell and visit, offering us some of the honey candy she'd made from the hives behind her house. She'd lure us with the candy and hornswoggle us into helping her with some chores. None of us minded. Today she didn't look up, just kept on working. Her white ceramic candy bowl sat on the railing. Normally the candy was piled above the rim. Today, I couldn't see if the bowl contained any candy at all.

Perhaps James was right, and maybe Mrs. Kelley felt it too. The environment seemed to have changed. The color of the sky and the trees and flowers were slightly muted. The air was deathly still. The breeze had stopped its musical soughing through the tree boughs. No birds sang. No dogs barked.

MERCIFULLY, WE GAVE THE MCEWEN HOUSE A WIDE BERTH and moved up Bridge Street. None of us said anything and no one else seemed to be about. The sinking feeling James had planted in me grew like a weed as we passed through empty streets and past deserted porches.

The bells of St. Paul's startled me as they suddenly rang out. Their clanging echoed off the walls of buildings and houses. The Episcopal Church followed suit. *Church*, I thought. *It must be Sunday. They're all in church.* The bells dismissed everyone and the streets soon filled with Franklinites donning their Sunday best.

"Are Ma and Pa at church?" I asked James.

"Nah, Pa had a fight with Frank."

This made me smile as I pictured my father and our

ornery horse, Frank, duking it out over whether or not old Frank would allow Pa to hitch him to the wagon.

"You know how those two quarrel," James said. "Besides, Ma was waiting to see if you'd come home."

"I don't know why she worries so," I said.

TWO

"Vitus Swinggate, you smell to high heaven," Mr. Whitton hollered.

"I've been told."

"Why do you have to come into my store reeking of dead fish, animal blood, and God only knows what else? I'm surprised there aren't any vultures following you. Can you, for once, have the common courtesy of washing off before entering a business establishment?"

"Sorry Mr. Whitton," I returned. "James dragged all us boys to town with him. I had only just gotten back from an expedition."

Mr. Whitton fanned his nose. "You and your expeditions, son. You really think you're Daniel Boone, don't you?"

I pulled my copy of *Biographical Memoir of Daniel Boone* by Timothy Flint from my haversack. I shook the tattered old book my father had given me years before. The soft and faded pages flapped back and forth like a bat's wings. "Yes, sir. I believe we're kindred spirits."

"You even have those silly pants that he wore," Mr. Whitton said as he pointed at my greasy buckskins. In the back of the store, James and George laughed at something James was holding.

"My pa made me these buckskins," I countered. "He and I killed the very deer that once wore this hide. He and I tanned the leather ourselves. I usually only wear them on hunting expeditions."

"I know that about you, Vitus. I've heard the story a dozen times if I've heard it once. I'm just giving you a hard time." He swept a pile of seeds from the counter into his hand. "Well, did you have any luck on your latest hunting excursion?"

"Trapping."

"Excuse me, son."

"I was trapping this time." I flipped open my haversack again and pulled out two otter pelts, still glistening on the inner side. "Took me a few days, but I got em. Gonna see if I can't sell them at Rainey's."

"Dear God, son!" Mr. Whitton reeled, waving his hand. "Get those out of here!"

"Just a second."

I studied the chess board on the small table by the display window.

"Just make your move will ya?" Mr. Whitton said. "And get your smelly behind out of here."

I moved the rook. "There," I said. "I'll leave your fine establishment now."

"You know you're welcome here, just do me the favor of not coming directly after one of your hunts, er, I mean expeditions."

A new book on the shelf beside the door caught my eye. *A Botanical Reference of Field and Forest, Flora and Fauna of Tennessee.* "You got a new book!" I said with guarded excitement. My brother and George loved to give me grief about being a book hound. Bibliophile, I call it. Most of my cohorts hadn't taken too much to reading, but when Mayor McEwen and his wife offered reading lessons, I was all over it like stink on a boar.

"Yes, sir," Mr. Whitton said. "Just got it in on Tuesday. You can look at it next time you're in here." He shooed me toward the door. "When you're clean."

I conceded. "Yes, sir."

The bell on the door jingled as I stepped onto the planked walkway outside. Chester sat on the steps basking in the sun, picking his nose. I sat beside him, laying my pelts out to dry. He jerked his finger from his nose. "Hey, pard," he said.

THE SHARP NOTES OF BUGLES CUT THROUGH THE QUIET village, puncturing the ever-present clomping of horses, squeaking wagon wheels, and polite conversations of passersby. Heads of the people around the square swiveled east, knowing the source of the sound would be obstructed by buildings, but looking anyway.

"It came from that direction," Chester said as he pointed toward the railroad.

"What's it mean?" I asked.

"Dunno."

The bell on the door of Whitton's jingled behind us as James flew through it, George in tow.

"It's happening, boys!" James yelled. "I told you something was about to happen!"

They both jumped off the walkway onto the muddy street, George yelling, "Yee haw," in flight.

"Let's go!" I said as I grabbed Chester's sleeve, giving it an upward yank. "It's happening!"

"What's happening?"

"I don't know. Something's happening and I'm not going to miss it."

We bolted off the steps in pursuit of our brothers who were drawn to the sound like sailors to sirens. The bugles led us to Rainey's Store by the railroad where a cluster of young men had formed. The Carter brothers stood tall in front, addressing the eager boys.

Chester and I clung to the sleeves of our big brothers' shirts as they picked through the crowd to the front. Moscow Carter stood erect on the top step wearing a captain's kepi. "We can wait no longer, boys!" he hollered.

The small crowd threw their fists into the air and hollered in consensus. Moscow, waiting on the cheers to abate, rubbed the scar on his cheek—a memento from the war with Mexico.

His younger brother, Theodrick, waved his hands to restore quiet.

"We can't wait for the war to come to us!" Moscow yelled. "We have to go to it!"

More cheers from the group.

"We can't allow bloodshed in our peaceful little town. Enlist today. Join Tod and me in the fight against northern aggression."

"Mock!" my brother yelled over the din of shouting. "We want to join!" He grabbed George to show they were the *we* he spoke of.

Chester and I shoved close to be included. I didn't want to stay here twiddling my thumbs while all the action happened.

"Sorry, boys." Moscow looked down at all four of us. "Your pa and I go way back. I can't let you go."

"But Mock," my brother protested. "What about the two of us?" His pointer finger wagging back and forth between himself and George.

"Sorry boys," Moscow said. "It's more important that you fellas stay here and protect our town."

"That's poppycock!" my brother yelled as he kicked the bottom riser of Rainey's steps.

Moscow bent to speak face to face with James. "War ain't pretty." He pointed at the scar on his face. "You know as well as I do, James. Look at your father."

"I'll just sneak off later," James threatened.

"Me too," I found myself saying. "The four of us can go on our own." I couldn't fathom why I was saying what I was saying, but I said it nonetheless.

Mock half snarled. "James, go home. Go home and have a good look at the way your pa walks now. Then tell me it's a good idea for you to join the cause."

"This is different," James protested. "This is our land.

This is our home. It's not Mexico! And we ain't fighting Indians either!"

Mock pointed west, his face turning red with anger. "Go on, boys. Get outta here before we have our own little war right here."

I can't speak for my company, but I shrank under Mock's glare. He was old enough to be our pa and was quite intimidating. James spat into the mud. George imitated him. They both turned and pushed through the crowd. I wanted to spit too, because my brother did, but Mock's expression swayed me to respectfully turn one-eighty and follow James and George.

Chester stared dumbfounded at Mock who had already engaged in a different conversation. I grabbed Chester's shoulder and directed him to move along.

"James, wait up!" I hollered. "I need to see if ole Rainey'll buy my pelts."

James shook his head without turning. Chester and I hurried to catch up.

Dejected and defeated, the four of us headed out of town, kicking stones, and grumbling the whole way.

"I can't believe that fart sniffer," George said.

"Hey, you shouldn't talk about Mr. Carter like that," Chester said. "He's like a pa to us."

"Well he ain't our pa," George said in return.

"I wish he was," Chester said. "Besides, maybe he's right."

George turned around. "What does he know?"

"He's a war hero, stupid." With that, George gave Chester a good thump on the back of the head.

James continued ahead of us staring at the ground. He hadn't said a word since we left Rainey's.

"Let's race," I said. No one responded. "To Campbell's pond. Last one's a rotten egg."

"Cut it out, Vitus," James said. "No one's in the mood for games."

"I'll give you a head start," I said, immediately regretting it.

"Don't patronize us, Vitus," James barked. "Just shut your bone box about racing."

"The dogwoods are blooming a little early this year," I said to change the subject.

"And we're not in the mood for one of your nature lectures either," James said.

"Ya'll wanna play Find the Indian?" I asked. It was our version of hide and seek. Pa resented the name we'd given the game. We didn't use it around him. More often than not, I was the Indian because of my buckskins. They almost never found me and usually gave up and left me in my hiding spot for hours. I'd eventually come home, greeted by James as if we had never played the game.

"Just shut up, Vitus!" James snapped at me as he marched on.

I clammed up and walked silently.

"Hi, boys!" Mrs. Kelley waved from her chair.

"Hi, Mrs. Kelley!" we all yelled in unison.

"Want some candy? Just made it yesterday."

"Not today, Mrs. Kelley," James answered for us all. He didn't miss a beat, just kept marching west.

I knew how important serving in the military was to James. Trying to get his approval and make him feel better,

I said, "Well, maybe we'll get our chance. Maybe the war will come to us. Then they can't stop us from fighting."

At that point, my dear friend, Chester said the wisest thing he would probably say in his entire life. "Be careful what you wish for, Vit."

THREE

SPRING 1862

The Invaders were coming. And soon.

The chirping and chattering of the forest stopped. Silence enveloped the northerly road.

Chills coursed up my spine.

A rumbling echoed through the hills in the north. A foul stench tainted the breeze. It would be only a matter of minutes.

A praying mantis crept into my field of vision. To the casual observer, the bug would have been lost in the budding leaves of the chestnut oak. It perched without a care on a twig preening itself like a cat, pulling its antennae through long, multi-hinged arms and combing its head with delicate claws.

The bug had no idea what approached us on the pike, blissfully unaware of the carnage and tragedy that would come with its arrival. And if it was bothered by my presence, it didn't show in its untroubled countenance.

The mantis's head pivoted back and forth. I followed

its gaze south where the pinnacle of the Hiram Masonic Lodge and the steeple of the Episcopal church peeked through the foliage a half mile away. To the north, the green insect and I had a clear view of the undulating pike to Nashville.

The marching army still hadn't come into view, so I watched the mantis stalk a small katydid like a lion would a gazelle. Its movements were methodical, mimicking young leaves oscillating in a gentle wind. Its long thorax took on the appearance of a twig and protruded from its miniature corn cob abdomen. The wings, like green husks, wrapped the body. The creature was completely camouflaged. It would've been difficult to distinguish it from its environment had I myself not become part of the tree. Creeping ever so slowly, the mantis closed distance on its unsuspecting quarry.

A faint haze lingered over the road to Nashville. The hillsides growing more obscured. The rumbling strengthened, pressing closer.

In a flash, the mantis snatched the katydid with its needle-like claws, impaling it. The mantis held fast as the katydid struggled unsuccessfully to free itself, but the bug could not escape the grasp of the larger predator. It eventually slowed its efforts to a stop.

The tree canopies erupted with fluttering as multitudes of birds suddenly took flight for safer havens.

Squirrels, chipmunks, and all manner of fauna skittered across the forest floor below me frantically searching for safety.

A small herd of deer darted between tree trunks, following the banks of the Harpeth to distant meadows.

Only Chester and I remained.

I shifted my weight in the branches, buzzing with energy.

The mantis still held its post. Almost as if singing a lullaby, it calmly watched its prey submit to the sleep of death. Its oversized head swiveled on an undersized neck surveying an entry point for its first bite. Its disproportionately large compound eyes rotated three hundred-sixty degrees checking every angle. Finding the sweet spot, the mantis sunk its imperceptible teeth into the katydid's neck. Tiny crunching sounds reported the progress made by the mandibles at cutting away at the neck.

The haze over the road grew into thick dust clouds. The smell of horse dung and stirred dirt rode the wind. A murder of crows took flight from the road and flew through the canopies around me, screeching their foreboding caws.

The katydid's head fell from the branch and tumbled through the air to the rutted road below. For several minutes, the crunching continued as the mantis devoured the katydid in its entirety.

As the dust thickened and rolled in my direction like a bank of storm clouds, my heart quickened and gooseflesh cropped up all over my body. The moment was finally upon us, and I had a front row seat. A position that would strike fear into a mother's heart and consume other boys with envy.

Chester was posted beside the road a hundred yards to the south, kneeling in chickweed and fastening stalks of cleavers to his shirt. He shrugged his shoulders questioningly. Raising my hand, I indicated he should hold his position a minute longer.

A church bell rang in town.

The earth began to quake like its crust would rupture. The tree limb I hugged vibrated. The mantis held firm to the trembling twig, eyes scanning.

Indistinct figures materialized on the road. I used the field glasses I'd "borrowed" from the Colonel's library for an appraisal. Horses, then men. Hundreds of cavalrymen and thousands of infantry coursed over the gentle hill on the Nashville Pike. A colossal blue army bore down on us, thousands of footfalls in lockstep thundering like a herd of bison. Flags and bayonets stabbed into the dusty air like a forest of pine trees.

I signaled to Chester, *ten thousand infantry, one thousand cavalry.* He nodded enthusiastically and sprinted across the bridge into Franklin. The bells of St. Paul's and the Episcopal Church rang with urgency. People poured from churches, shops, and homes to learn of the oncoming commotion. Chester ran through the gathering spectators and melted into the crowd.

An impossible number of cavalry passed under my dangling feet and thundered across the bridge, flowing into town like ants toward molasses. Thousands upon thousands of Invader infantry, sharply dressed in their blue uniforms and gold stars, with bright flags flying and bands playing, filed over the river, and spread throughout the streets until the town was blanketed in blue.

I held tightly to the shaking tree, awestruck. I'd never seen a Northern soldier before and we had been anticipating their arrival since they took Nashville a month before. Suddenly I was looking down on thousands of them just a dozen feet below my boots. Imposing as they were, many were talking and smiling.

I leveled an imaginary rifle at a soldier wiping his brow and pulled the trigger. He continued past, replacing his hat. I swung my invisible gun toward a young teenage boy who saw me and took up a pretend pistol and fired back. I shot an old man. He grabbed his heart and made a dramatic show of being hit. He flashed me a wink and carried on. Most of the others didn't notice me or just paid me no mind. The few that did, gave me a smile or a nod. A harmless little boy watching the parade of the mighty Union Army.

It seemed to take hours for the blue torrent to fully pass. When the bulk of it eventually disappeared into the southern countryside, the road became quiet again.

The mantis was gone.

I took leave of my perch and dog-trotted down the pike toward Franklin.

FOUR

Few Franklinites remained on the streets. Many of the Invaders had stayed behind and wandered up and down Main Street.

The square was clotted with wagons, horses, cannons, and ammunition caissons. I kept to the walkway in front of the businesses. Men in blue coats were trying on hats in Mr. Glass's shop. Three were in the dress shop; one of them holding a dress in front of himself prancing around. Another squeezed the chest of the dress, both laughed.

In front of the opera house, an Invader harassed a performer, asking her, "How much, honey?"

"This is an *opera* house!" she said as she shrugged herself free from one's grip and stormed off. The law offices, bank, and post office were closed up tight. Through the large display window of Whitton's General Store, I could see bluebellies perusing the aisles, pocketing products. Mr. Whitton sat behind the counter with his eyes cast downward.

An Invader bumped into me as he exited the door. I held my tongue and stepped inside. Mr. Whitton's eyes were wide. His pupils jerked toward the door, directing me to leave.

"Hello, Mr. Whitton," I said, my voice a little creaky. My eyes, out of habit, darted to the chessboard sitting on a small table by the display window. The black queen still had the white king in check.

Mr. Whitton jerked his head toward the street, urging me to get a move on.

An Invader poured what was left of the coffee beans into his coat pocket. His comrade wiped his face with a bolt of cloth hanging on display.

"How can I help you...young man?" Mr. Whitton stuttered, feigning normalcy.

Two Invaders, standing near the garden tools, turned to look at me. Sweat gathered on my forehead and my stomach turned. Did they know I was the kid in the tree? That I had counted their numbers? That I'd sent Chester to Mr. Carter with information about their army?

I didn't want to leave for fear of looking suspicious. I leaned against the heavy wooden counter.

"I need a pound of lard, a sack of table salt, and half a pound of coffee," I said.

I confirmed the coins Ma had given me were still in my pocket. Whitton's General Store had been a regular part of my life for as long as I could remember. Ma used to bring me here as a child. Once I had turned eight years old, I was deemed responsible enough to carry out errands on my own. Once a week, she'd give me money to pick up supplies while I was in town for school.

If I didn't smell like a wild animal, Mr. Whitton let me stay to read from the small collection of books he kept in stock (like the one an Invader presently flipped through). I spent hours reading and re-reading anything on wildlife and botany.

A couple Invaders spoke to one another about a coffee grinder. "It'd be nice to have one of these in our saddle bag."

"You're right about that."

They held an accent that almost sounded foreign. They spoke the same language we did in the South, but it was hurried and clipped. Their use of vowels differed from mine. Shorter, harder. It struck me strange that our enemy didn't speak a foreign tongue like the Indians or the French.

Mr. Whitton nervously worked on my order, sweat poured over his face. An Invader brushed past me toward the front and mindlessly moved the chess pieces around on the game board. A hot storm gathered behind my eyes.

For the better part of two years, I'd been playing chess with a mystery opponent. When Mr. Whitton had first displayed the game, I decided to move a black pawn two squares forward. The next time I came in, a white pawn had been moved. A war had begun between us. Weekly, I'd make a purchase for Ma and make another move. Upon my next visit, the mystery opponent would've made his move.

Mr. Whitton wouldn't reveal who was playing with me and had promised not to disclose my identity either. He assured me it wasn't him. He said he had no earthly idea how to play. The only person I knew that could play was

Mayor McEwen. He had taught me in his library. But his tactical style differed from my mystery opponent.

Over the months, my adversary and I had each won twice. Just a week before, I had positioned my queen to put him in check. It was clear my playmate didn't have a chance to get himself out of it either. And now he never would. The stupid bluebelly Invader had moved everything around.

"That's forty-two cents, son," Mr. Whitton said.

I returned the chess pieces to their proper places. I handed Mr. Whitton the coins in my pocket and stepped outside. Chester was making his way toward the courthouse through the crowded walkway in front of the feed store.

I crossed the road and found him sitting on the courthouse steps chewing on a piece of straw.

"Hey, pard," he said.

"Did you tell Mr. Carter everything?" I asked.

"Yeah."

"And?" I said, prodding him to add to the story. Sometimes Chester wasn't big on finishing a thought or stringing together words in an intelligible, communicative way. He was a lot of great things, but Tennyson he was not.

"I tol 'em what you tol me."

"Then what happened?"

"Well, what do you think, Vit? He tol the Rebs. I believe they retreated south."

Mr. Fountain Branch Carter commissioned our scouting job to inform a small contingent of the Louisiana cavalry who were camped just south of the Carter home. They were only four hundred strong, so I wasn't surprised they retreated.

"Here's your five cents." He handed me a half dime.

I clapped his shoulder. "Well, we did all we could. Good job, buddy. Let's get to the McEwen house."

FIVE

John McEwen
mayor of Franklin
1861-1865

We weaved through blue coats and sweaty horses and made our way to Mayor McEwen's house to see what he knew. The McEwen house was a beacon of strength and comfort. An imposing brick building stretching to a height and width double what other houses were. The narrow windows of the second floor seemed to glare like angry eyes down on Fair Street.

The boys and I called it a mansion, but Mrs. McEwen insisted it was a simple house. We knew better. In fact, we'd had foot races around the perimeter of it. It took the better part of twenty seconds to circumnavigate the hulking structure. I knew it was a fancy house, though. Mrs. McEwen took us kids on a tour around the place one afternoon, giving us an architecture lesson. She used words like arched windows, corniced eaves, Italianate features, and all sorts of other architectural jargon.

It had covered porches everywhere. A porch in the

front, one on the side, another in the back. The ornate roofs over the porches were supported by dramatic arches held by Corinthian-style columns linked together with railings of heavy, ornate spindles.

Strangers in blue coats paced the front porch and two horses, trampling the flower beds, were tied to a magnolia by the front walkway. We slowed our gait and angled to the right of the house to avoid the sentries on the front porch.

One of the Yankees watched us like a hawk. He sat on the railing, leaning against a column. He had a purple birthmark on his right cheek that resembled a giant tick crawling from his thick black beard to escape the sun under his forage cap.

His head pivoted like the praying mantis, and his beady eyes glared.

An old magnolia pod crunched under my feet, almost rolling my ankle. I pulled my attention away from the awful man on the porch and followed the shade of the trees to the back porch. The usual crowd of boys gathered on the floor in the parlor, playing games and ignoring our arrival.

"Where's Mayor McEwen?" I asked a kid named Roger. He gave me no response.

The McEwen's servant, who we called Mammy, was in the kitchen standing on a three-legged stool, wiping coal soot from a white and blue vase. The finish on the cast iron stove had been freshly cleaned and oiled. Embroiled in Spring cleaning, she didn't notice me sliding by.

The front room was empty of occupants. An Invader walked past the window obscured by the lace curtain, but his boots thumped on the wooden porch planks. A mannequin stood in the window's light with strips of flowered fabric hanging over its shoulders. Mrs. McEwen's sewing machine had recently been vacated, having been stopped mid-seam. A panel of cloth hung from it like a windless flag. Her latest addition of *Godey's Lady's Book* sat on a wingback chair, opened to a full-page fashion plate containing the pattern for the dress she had been working on.

The door to the library was closed. I walked on tiptoes toward it while Chester stayed behind to join in a game of jacks. I set my groceries down and flattened myself on the heartwood pine floor where I inched toward the small opening beneath the door. The slight smell of mildew wafted from the cellar through a knot hole in a plank near the threshold.

Soft voices and a cool breeze from inside the library squeezed their way under the door. I saw several pairs of feet. Some stationary, some pacing slightly, but all had trousers and dirty boots. Scooting around on my side like a legless dog trying to scratch its back on cobblestone, I changed the angle of observation through the crack.

Off to the side of the room, two pairs of lady feet hung from the sofa near the bay window, one in formal shoes and stockings under the hem of a formal dress. The other pair, smaller and bare, was swinging above the rug.

The voices were a little muffled, and the racket the boys were making in the parlor made it difficult to understand everything being discussed, but it sounded as if the mayor was in some kind of trouble.

"Vitus Swinggate!" I heard a booming voice from the

hallway behind me. I recognized it before my surname shot out of her mouth. Mammy. "Whad you think you doin', boy?"

"Well, I…"

"Git up off dat floor."

"Yes, ma'am."

She grabbed my arm and gave it an upward wrench, pulling me to my feet and nearly dislocating my humerus from its socket. Mammy was very strong. I was big for my age, and she could still toss me around like a rag doll.

"Go on now, ya here? Mind yo own."

"Yes, ma'am." Head hanging, I started toward the parlor. Mammy was close behind. Before I could join the other kids, she grabbed my right arm, pinching the skin, and swung me around. Because I was taller than most twelve-year-olds, we were eye to eye. "Whad you hear?"

"Nothing, Mammy. You yanked me off the floor before I could get the full intelligence."

She gave me a little push toward the parlor. "Never mind."

I tried playing jacks with the rest of the group, but I had a rather difficult time peeling my eyes from the library door. I bounced the ball and before I could catch it, the door cracked open. Out of the corner of my eye, I saw the ball fall to the floor and roll between Roger's knees. "You lose!"

His comment didn't faze me in the least because I suddenly had a greater focus than winning a stupid game of jacks. Mayor McEwen's daughter, Addie, squeezed through the gap in the door as if it and the frame were giant jaws trying to close on her and bite her in half. Extricating herself from the library so that no one could see what lied within, she pulled the door closed and started across the hall toward the staircase. Dull thuds ascended the rise as she ran up the steps.

I hopped up off the floor and started to follow her, but the library door opened again, stopping me in my tracks. This time it was Mrs. McEwen.

"Oh, hi, Vitus," she said with a hint of distress. Her hands folded on her stomach and her spine perfectly straight, she made every effort to remain stoic.

"Hi Mrs. McEwen," I returned. "I was just…is everything okay?"

Her hands slid down her dress, chasing wrinkles that may have cropped up from her time on the couch. Her composure seemed fragile.

"Oh, never you mind, darlin'."

She began to walk away but stopped abruptly and turned back around. "Say, Vitus, why don't you accompany Adelicia to the forest to collect some mushrooms for me. We're having unexpected company for dinner tonight and it would be a big help."

"Yes, ma'am." My heart raced at the prospect.

"Besides, I think it would be good for her to get some fresh air."

I didn't move from my position as I watched her climb the stairs. A minute later small, bare feet appeared under the bottom of the banister. They slowly and deliberately descended the stairs. Addie was barefoot a lot. Not because she couldn't afford shoes like some of the boys that boarded at her home, but because it was her way of feeling normal. She spent a lot of time with boys like me, and she sometimes felt alienated in her expensive dresses and clean shoes.

To please her parents, she spoke like a lady and practiced the manners of her class, but she enjoyed the activities normally associated with boys just as much as I did.

Soft, brown hair covered her downcast face as she passed family portraits above the stairs. Nearing the foot of the staircase, she kicked the bottom of her dress with her shins as she lifted her feet like a toy soldier. She jumped the last two risers and landed softly on the balls of her feet on the heartwood.

"Hey, Vit," she said when she noticed me. Her voice was a little shaky, and her smile was forced. She flew past me toward the kitchen, grabbed a deep, wicker basket, and shot out the door.

She was still on the back porch when I caught up with her. The basket handle rested in the crook of her elbow.

"You ready to hunt mushrooms?" she said, staring into the backyard. Before I could answer, she bounced down the steps into the grass. Her pace was quick as she headed toward the woods, her white dress floating behind her. Her hair, somehow always clean and shiny, bounced at her shoulders, and the scent of scent of cinnamon oil carried on the breeze. I took long, hurried steps to stay astride.

"Do you want to talk about it?" I asked.

Her emerald eyes remained forward.

"Nope."

Slightly defeated, I fell in line behind her as we crossed the road and entered the forest where we followed the well-worn trail that wound through the oaks and hickories. She glanced energetically into the understory as she strolled. Normally we'd be playing tag or competing in some fashion, but today she was different. Quiet. Pensive.

"Well you're going to have to tell me sooner or later what's wrong," I said after several minutes of quiet. She continued to march along, wordless.

"Can you at least tell me what we're hunting?"

"Mushrooms."

"Well I know that, Addie. Care to specify?"

"Morels," she said.

We searched wordlessly for fungus. Eventually I found a grouping of morels at the base of a dead oak.

We collected a dozen mushrooms and sat together on a damp log. Her face showed the rumination she conducted. Finally she broke the silence.

"I don't think Daddy's the mayor anymore."

I gave her another minute to deliberate without interruption.

"Vitus, the confounded Yankees want Daddy to surrender Franklin to them without a fight."

"Do you think he will?" My voice cracked.

"Yes, Momma said he would."

"That's horse crap!" I said without considering my words.

She raised an eyebrow. Letting her down stung me a little. She appreciated proper speech and had admitted she enjoyed my use of language more than the other boys. "Those other boys are so crass," she'd said. "I'm glad you can speak like a gentleman—at least you do around me."

"We need to fight," I said. "They can't just come in and take our town!"

"Think about it, Vitus. If we fight, Franklin could be destroyed and a lot of us could be killed."

I gave it some consideration, then said, "I guess you're right. I guess Mayor…your dad, realizes that too."

"He'll surrender peacefully, Vitus. He doesn't want to see his town torn to shreds."

She was quiet for a moment.

"Father even had Jennie and me sing a song for the Northern men. You believe that?"

We spoke no more about it as we walked toward her home. There was a discernible difference in the forest as we walked the path. What it was, I couldn't quite pin down. A smell, a feeling. The forest's mood had changed somehow.

A figure appeared ahead. The shape of a man seemed to materialize from thin air at the trail head looking into the forest as if waiting for us. It was a silhouette I didn't recognize. He was too tall to be one of the kids and a good bit thinner than Mayor McEwen.

Addie, noticing the figure, was startled, and hooked her arm around mine.

"Who is that man?"

We slowed our pace.

"I don't know."

"He's just staring at us," she said. "Why?"

I didn't answer. I was too nervous. Something about his posture. The way his hands hung out to the side, motionless. His upper back had a slight incline as if peering through the understory at us. He had a Yankee forage cap and a long coat.

As we closed distance, I could see that it was the scary

man from the front porch. The one with the ugly birthmark on his face. The man who glared at Chester and me. His eyes were fixed on us now and held a twinkle of evil. They were piercing and appeared yellow. Like a rattlesnake's.

"What are youin's doing out here?" His voice was calm and raspy.

"Excuse me sir, but it's not any of your concern," Addie said. She pulled me to speed our gait and navigate around him.

"Whoa, there," he said. "What's the big hurry?" The man with the horrible birthmark grabbed Addie's arm, pulling her to him. "I just wanted to talk to you."

"We don't want to talk to you!" As Addie said this, she slapped him on the side of his head with the wicker basket. The mushrooms scattered with little thumps into the surrounding leaf litter.

The man laughed as his viper face swung back around. "Spunky little lady, huh?"

"Leave her alone, you stupid bluebelly!" I yelled before I had given it any thought.

The man's nose crinkled, making the purple tick on his face crawl. His eyes squinted and lips curled. As fast as lightning, he gave Addie a shove and grabbed me by the shirt with both hands. He lifted me from the ground until I was his eye level. I was like a helpless bunny staring into the eyes of a snake. The devil himself.

The devil's breath smelled something awful. Like rotten eggs, tobacco spit, and horse's butt, all rolled up into one heinous odor.

"What did you say, boy?" Spittle hit my lips and chin. I wanted to vomit. I don't know where the courage had come from, possibly from dealing with bullies all my life. None of which had been as formidable as the one who now held me off the ground.

"Keep your dirty hands off her." My voice squeaked as the words forced themselves across my vocal cords by the will of some force outside myself. It was not of my volition that I defended Addie's honor, but something else.

His face contorted in a mixture of anger and amusement. With a great shove, he tossed me to the floor of broken acorns and ferns.

The fall had knocked the breath out of me. Struggling to breathe, I looked up at my attacker as he spit about a gallon of tobacco on my face and chest. Anger grew in me so fast and so fervently that the heat in my face probably boiled off some of the rank saliva.

"You ugly, stupid bluebelly Yankee son of a sow! You're a coward!" I regretted saying it before the stream of words penetrated his simple brain. A murderous scowl took shape as he bent toward me. I coiled up, ready to kick him, but something caught his attention. A voice. Someone was calling after him from the McEwen house.

"I'll deal with the two of you later," he said through gritted teeth. He pushed Addie to the side with one hand, sending her to hands and knees as he stormed up the trail toward the voice. I helped her to her feet and guided her to her family's large, stone well. "I'm gonna get that guy," I said as I primed the pump.

"Just forget about it, Vitus," she said.

I splashed well water on my face to clean the Yankee spit off my cheeks. It was a persistent filth; I wasn't sure I'd succeeded in removing all of it. It probably needed scouring with hot water like Mammy's pots.

On the porch, I told Addie I was sorry she'd lost her mushrooms.

"It's all right. It's the least of our worries today. Thanks for protecting my honor back there."

She stood on her tiptoes to give me a little peck on the cheek, careful to avoid the foul residual devil-spit. Luckily she went inside before she could see me blush. All the boys poured out the door onto the planks of the porch, pushing and cajoling.

I grabbed Chester's sleeve. "Where's everyone going?"

"Mrs. McEwen said we all had to either go home tonight or sleep out here on the porch."

"Why's that?"

"Cause the Yankees are stayin' here tonight."

"What about the McEwens?" My eyes darted back and forth looking for the man with the birthmark.

"Ya mean, what about Addie, huh, Vit?"

"No, I mean all of them.," I said. "Are they getting kicked out too?"

"Nah, they can stay, but we gotta go."

"Permanently?" The worry was obvious in my tone.

"Don't think so. I think it's just a day or two. Shoot, Vit, I don't know what they're doin'."

"Are you going home?"

"Whatn't plannin' on it. Was just gonna stay out on the porch with the fellas."

"Well, I need to go home," I said. "Come with me."

"Why?"

"I'll tell you on the way."

"Okay, pard. I'll come along."

"Hold on," I said as I ran in the back door. Mammy was scrubbing black residue off a copper pot. My sack of groceries was nowhere to be found. "Mammy, have you seen my groceries?"

She didn't look up from her work. "Probaly at the sto."

"Funny, Mammy. You know what I mean."

"They should be where you lef em."

"They're not," I said, heat forming behind my eyes.

"Things like that don't just up and crawl away." She hung the pot by the handle above the iron cooking range.

"You're a big help, Mammy. Pa is going to tan my hide."

I met Chester on the porch again. We shot down the back steps and ran toward the lane that led west toward our houses in the country. As we walked, I kept a look out for the man with the birthmark. I told Chester what had happened in the woods and he agreed it was the smarter move not to hang around the McEwen house for a day or two.

SIX

Mrs. Kelley's blue clapboard house was usually very welcoming. But today, an Invader sat backward in her ladder-backed chair. He'd dragged it out into the yard and the oak legs dug into the mud as he rocked back and forth. One of his cohorts told an off-color joke and his laughter tore at the air. Mrs. Kelley was nowhere to be seen.

Along the road just outside of town, Yankee camps had been erected. The quiet country road was consumed by the racket. Men in blue uniforms stood around campfires drinking and yammering in their weird accent. Hammers banged as they pounded tent spikes. Horses pulled at their yokes to reach new grass. Spoons clinked against pans. The smell of coffee, wood smoke, and horse dung lingered as we continued up the road wordlessly. I'm not sure either one of us knew what to say.

Chester and I parted ways at his yard and I continued toward the hills in the west. Before I was to my house, muffled shouts from inside made it to my ears. A section of a freshly felled tree, still attached to the yoke, lay in the front yard. A long gouge in the earth stretched from the forest to the end of the tree. Our workhorse, Frank was tied to the hitch.

James was leaning against the washbasin in the kitchen when I opened the back door. His face was red with anger. His eyes, wet with tears, flicked toward me, then back at my parents who were seated at the small table.

Before hearing any words exchanged, I knew what the yelling was about. James and my folks had been arguing since the Carter brothers enlisted the year before.

Moscow and Theodrick Carter had recruited nearly two dozen boys that day at Rainey's store. Ten days later, their company was sworn into service at Camp Trousdale and designated the title Company H.

Francis Watkins Carter, or Wad, had joined Company D a week or two before Moscow and Theodrick, tearing asunder the trio known around town as Tod, Wad, and Mock. At Camp Trousdale, they were reunited when Wad's company and nine others came together to form the Twentieth Tennessee Regiment, Volunteer Infantry, Confederate States Army.

With the fall of Nashville and the subsequent invasion of our stomping grounds, the quarrel between James and our parents had come to a head.

"George is going!" James yelled.

"I don't care what George is doing," my dad said. "He ain't my son. You are."

"What's going on?" I asked. No one answered. As if I hadn't come in at all.

"Where's George going?" I fastened the door behind me as I stepped fully into the room.

"Grandaddy was a soldier!" said James. "Pa fought for his country!"

"And look where it got me, son! In case you forgot, I'm a cripple now."

"This is malarky!" James yelled as he stamped across the floor, bumping my arm on his way outside. The door slammed, knocking Ma's sampler off the wall.

"Ma, please tell me what's going on."

I was only a ghost.

"He's gonna go anyway, ya know?" Pa said.

"How can you say that?" Ma said, blinking away tears.

"Any red-blooded, abled-body man is gonna go. Hell, I'd be the first to join up if I weren't a cripple."

Ma covered her mouth with her hands as if she was going to vomit. Tears splattered on the floor when she bowed her head. The parched wood soaked them up like a sieve. "I'm not letting my boy get himself killed."

She stood and left the house. She paused in the dooryard, as if to gather her thoughts, then slid her forearm across her eyes and started off in search of James.

PA MADE ME HELP HIM WITH THE LUMBERJACK DUTIES THAT had been interrupted. We took Frank back to the woods and rigged him up with another section of the tree and dragged it back. Pa had hoped to extend the split rail fence and buy another horse.

"I just don't have the gumption to do any more today, Vitus," Pa said. "Tomorrow we'll start splitting it into fence rails."

I didn't see James or Ma for the rest of the evening. I was in a deep sleep when James shook me awake.

"Vitus, wake up a minute."

"What is it? Why you waking me up in the middle of the night?"

He sat on the mattress beside me, the ropes squeaking under the weight.

"I'm leaving."

"Leaving? Where are you going?"

"Me and George are joining the cause."

I sat up in bed. "The cause?"

"We're leaving tonight. Moscow Carter told us where to go to meet up with Company H."

"Mock?" I said in a daze. "How'd you talk to him?"

"I don't have time for this now, but he's home."

"He is?"

"I gotta go, Vit."

"Where's that?" I said. Tears beginning to well.

"Listen. I don't know where we're going, but I need you to promise me you'll stay here and take care of Ma and Pa. Can you do that?"

I nodded my head pathetically.

"Honor bright, Vitus?"

I nodded again.

"Say it Vit. Say you'll stay here and take care of them. And keep getting educated. You're the smartest person I know. Make something special of yourself, or I'll be quite disappointed."

"Honor bright," I said meekly.

"I know you, Vit, you're gonna wanna follow me."

"I won't." I looked at the floor.

He put his hand on my shoulder. "I know you want to fight these bluebellies as bad as I do, but you're too young. You've got too much smarts, Vitus. It'd be a shame for your clever brains to get shot out."

"I'm not too young—"

"Listen. Ma and Pa are going to need you. You'll be the man of the house. Take care of the farm. Protect it from the Yanks. Can you do that?"

"Yeah."

He leaned over and gave me a kiss on the forehead, something he's never even considered doing in all his life. The bed ropes squeaked again as he stood to his full height.

"Good luck, little buddy," he said. "And please don't tell Ma and Pa until morning. Give me some time to put some distance between us."

He quietly pulled the door behind himself, latching the door quietly. Tears dripped onto my pillow. There was an undeniable feeling in my stomach that told me I'd never see my brother again.

SEVEN

The next morning I had a strip of bacon for breakfast in the empty kitchen. Ma and Pa were nowhere to be found, so I met Chester at Campbell pond. Each of us were in somber moods. Little was said, but we both knew what the other was thinking.

We chucked rocks in the water for a few minutes, avoiding talk about our brothers' departure.

"Let's go to the McEwen house," I said.

"Why? I thought we were going to stay away from there."

"I'm worried about Addie. I'm afraid that bluebelly turd is going to do something to her."

"All right. Let's do it."

I could always count on Chester. He'd do just about anything I'd ask.

In town, Invaders milled about and citizens were hidden or gone. The McEwen house looked as it always did. A beacon of sanctuary. White sheets and large undergarments hung on clotheslines, flopping in the breeze. Mammy preferred her clothes to be hung dry. "They smell like spring that way," she had said. "Besides, pressin', starchin', and ironin' the family's clothes is enough work nohow." We hopped up the back steps and entered the kitchen without knocking.

Mammy was in the laundry closet running the McEwens' clothes through the heavy rollers of the drying press.

"Hi, Mammy. Do you know where Addie is?"

"Front porch," she murmured as she straightened her tired back.

The house was quieter than I'd ever heard it. The grandfather clock ticked from the library as we passed down the corridor toward the front porch. The ceiling squeaked a few times indicating the McEwen girls moving in their upstairs room.

Addie was sitting on the porch railing and Mayor McEwen was rocking in a chair. Both were staring at something across the street.

Chester and I stepped outside. Mayor McEwen noticed us first.

"Hi, boys."

"Hello, sir," we said in unison.

"I heard about your brothers."

"How did you know, sir?" I asked.

"Fountain Branch Carter was here this morning for our weekly coffee. He said Moscow was secretly recruiting more boys and sending them along to the 20th Regiment."

I looked at Addie. She turned and gave me a sweet smile.

"Don't get any ideas, boys. I told Mr. Carter that Moscow shouldn't be bothering boys your age."

He and Addie both returned their attention to the point of interest across the street.

"They treat their horses as poorly as they do us," Mayor McEwen said.

A horse, tied to a low tree limb in the yard of St. Paul's, stomped and whinnied. A man, with his back to us was trying to adjust the saddle. When the horse moved, as one might naturally do, the man kicked it in the knee.

"Sit still!" he yelled.

This only agitated the horse more. With each protest of the abuse, the man hurled profanities and threw punches at its withers and kicks at its belly.

"He's abusing that horse, Daddy," Addie said. "Can't you do anything?"

"I'm afraid not, darling. Not anymore."

Addie turned toward me. "You know who that is, Vitus? That's the man from the forest. The one with the ugly birthmark on his face. I told Daddy all about it."

My blood boiled.

The horse jerked its head from the man's grip. A white lightning bolt blaze on its muzzle flashed back and forth.

Not wanting to get into it at the moment, Mayor McEwen pushed himself out of his chair. "Boys, I'm glad you're here. There's something I need to talk you about. Please join me in the library." He held the door open and let us enter the house before him.

"Addie, stay out here and keep an eye on that scoundrel," the Mayor said. "Only disturb us if it's something to do with him."

"Yes, sir."

In the library, Mayor McEwen sat us down and explained to us that he was no longer the mayor. That he thought peace was the best option for the town of Franklin. He went on to say that he'd do whatever it took to keep our town from being destroyed and the streets from running red with blood.

A man of his status, despite the occupation of the Northerners, had several cards to play to protect his town. And apparently, he planned to take advantage of the boys under his tutelage.

"I am asking, not recruiting, not forcing, but *asking* all you boys under my roof to help me keep an eye on this town and protect it. Don't get excited, you won't be bearing arms or engaging in battle. But you'll be doing something more important."

"What's more important than that, sir?" I asked.

"If you're willing, I'd like to use the two of you as scouts."

"Scouts?"

"Yes, scouts. Spies if you will."

Chester and I looked at each other with enthusiastic grins.

"What that means is, you'll be keeping an eye on the Northerners, gathering intelligence, and reporting it back to me."

"Like we done yesterday?" Chester asked.

"Precisely. You did a great job yesterday. We knew that was coming, but it was you all who alerted the Rebels of the numbers. Because of you, they knew not to engage, but to retreat instead. Most importantly, you kept bloodshed out of our town. This is what I need you to help me do from here on out. Can you do it?"

"Yes, sir," we said simultaneously.

"What about the other boys?" I asked.

"I've recruited Roger and Sam and two girls from the Institute."

"Girls?" Chester said.

"Yes, girls. Their names are Lillian and Annie. They're just as capable at espionage as boys."

"Is that all, sir?" I asked

"Yes. Every other boy is either off fighting, too yellow-bellied, or have over-protective parents. So there's six of you in my spy ring, three teams. But this is top secret, you understand? You can't even discuss it amongst the other teams."

We both nodded understanding.

"Your job is to keep an eye on the Yankees; it's also going to be your job to do the opposite."

Our heads tilted together in confusion. Reading our body language, the Mayor continued, "I need you to let me know when units of Rebel guerrillas are planning an attack on the occupying Northerners."

"Why's that, sir?"

"As I said before, I want our town to survive this conflict unscathed. If you boys catch wind of an impending raid, I have a small contingent of volunteer soldiers who have agreed to make every effort to turn them away."

"So you have Confederates who are rebels against the Confederate Rebels?" I said.

"Well, sort of. To keep it simple—" his voice lowered to

a whisper as he cupped one side of his mouth—"and between us; there are sympathizers in the area who don't fall exactly in line with the North or the South. Like me, they don't believe in this war and are willing to go to certain lengths to avoid having it on our soil."

Our heads bobbed up and down.

"Just go about your normal lives as much as possible. Go hunting. Go fishing. Do whatever you do. The only difference is you keep an eye out for soldiers. If you see a group of bluecoats larger than ten forming in town, come see me. If soldiers from the Union or Confederate Army approach town, hightail it straight to me. You understand?"

"Yes, sir."

"Don't speak of this to anyone. Not your parents, not the other boys, not Mrs. McEwen, not even Addie. Also, I don't want you to share anything with Fountain Branch Carter any longer. His emotions are getting the better of him. He's a dear, dear friend, but I'm afraid we don't share the notion of keeping violence out of this town. So don't go to him anymore about intelligence.

"Keep a low profile. Just act like kids. Don't look suspicious. Come to and fro like normal. We'll still be having classes. If you have something to report, give me a sign, and I'll call you into the library. We'll make like you're in trouble for something—which isn't a far stretch, is it boys?"

"What's the sign?"

"I'll come out and check on you all during your lessons. When you see me, both of you cross your arms. That'll let me know to call you in. Does that work?"

"Yes, sir."

"That's all for now. Go about your business as usual."

"Yes, sir."

We got up to leave, but I stopped.

"Sir?"

"Yes, son."

"How is it that Moscow Carter is home?"

"Moscow was captured at the Battle of Mill Springs in January and was released on parole and given permission to serve it out at home."

"Any word on Tod and Wad?"

"No. I suppose you could ask Moscow."

"Thank you."

A WEEK LATER, CHESTER AND I FOUND MOSCOW AND HIS father cutting limbs off a recently fallen tree near their large cotton gin. Tiny flakes of cotton floated through the air like a gentle snow.

"I'm anxious to get back out there and fight," Mock said when we asked about his recent capture and parole. "I'm waiting to see if I'm to be traded for a Union soldier."

Before we could ask, he shouldered his axe and said, "I don't know anything about your brothers, fellas. I told them where to head, but I didn't pressure them to leave. And no, I'm not telling you where they went."

"I didn't think you would," I said. "Have you heard anything from *your* brothers?"

"Actually, we just received some disheartening news. Wad's been wounded at Shiloh." He wiped sweat from his forehead. Fountain Branch Carter carried on working among the tall grass without looking up, hacking away at a stubborn stem in the crown of the tree.

"How bad is he?" Chester asked.

"Not sure yet."

"Sorry to hear that," I said, then looked at his father for a reaction.

Chester kicked at a patch of lichen on the trunk. "Anything about Tod?"

"Not as of yet." Mock swung his axe down hard on the trunk. "You boys are welcome to stop by another time for updates."

"Thank you, Mock," I said. "Bye, Mr. Carter," I called down the length of the tree to Fountain Branch. He threw up a hand without speaking.

Chester and I walked home quietly, meditating on the dangers of war. It was a heavy thing finding out a kid you grew up with was wounded on a distant battlefield.

In the following weeks, we watched as friends and neighbors sold their furniture, packed their essentials, and moved farther south. A cloud of fear descended upon the small town as more and more Federal outposts cropped up around town and increasing conflicts erupted between them and Rebel guerrilla fighters. All of which was reported to Colonel McEwen (we called him Colonel since he was no longer mayor) by his network of child spies.

There was an exodus of able-bodied men like my brother and George who traded their farm tools for rifles and joined the Confederate cause. Kids like me and the others at the McEwen house were left behind to pick up the slack on the farms and engage in espionage in our free time unbeknownst to our parents. Having the Invaders walk among us was unsettling, but it wasn't until the fall of 1862 the bloodshed Colonel McEwen feared came to town.

EIGHT

While the rest of the boys flung themselves to the floor, slithering under furniture, Chester and I sprang into action at the sound of artillery fire. Before the Colonel could snatch us by the collars and yank us into the cellar, we bolted out the back door and ran full chisel toward the Harpeth River.

We slid down the banks and scrambled along the waterline until we reached the double covered bridge connecting Franklin to the road to Nashville. We skittered across rocks to the north side of the river and crawled up the embankment to take our positions under the brush.

Ever since the Northern army occupied our town, we'd been watching the road to Nashville as the Colonel had instructed. We waited with great anticipation for the arrival of reinforcement troops, foraging parties, or skirmishes—anything to report to the Colonel. We'd hook a few bass from the bridge's shadow while we waited. From behind boulders or piles of flood debris along the banks, we'd watched as small contingents came and went across the bridge.

On quiet days, we'd climb the banks carrying driftwood rifles to scope out the Nashville Pike. We'd lay prone on either side of the road and fire our imaginary carbines at a pretend regiment of Yankee soldiers bearing down on us.

On that cold day in November, something big was happening and it wasn't pretend. A deep rumble, mixed with yelling and whinnying, grew to a roar as the shapes of men and horses came into view on the Nashville Pike.

A group of Rebel cavalry suddenly appeared from behind us and hurried across the bridge running up the road. A small number of infantry followed and spread out into the forest. There was a heated exchange of gunfire. We lay there dumbstruck as the sounds of battle grew louder and louder. The Rebels held their ground for longer than I imagined they could, but eventually had to pull back.

The Rebels continued sending volleys as they retreated back across the bridge. Chester and I slid down the bank and hid at the base of the bridge at the water's edge. The thumping footsteps and rumbling wagons on the planks above us gave me a rush. It pained me not to be a part of it. I popped off a few rounds with a stick rifle as gunfire was exchanged above our position. I counted the number of infantry, cavalry, and artillery pieces.

A man shrieked at the window opening above our position.

"Watch out!" Chester yelled.

I looked up just in time to see a gray mass falling toward me. Because of Chester's warning, I was able to throw myself out of the way. The body of a Confederate soldier hit the water beside me with a sickening thud and splash. His lower back hit the shallow rocks, upper body submerging in deeper, muddy water.

"Holy cow!"

Chester and I both jumped another pace back. If I had been an old man, I'm sure my heart would have burst.

The submerged head of the soldier bobbed, pressing his face above the water. His eyes, glassy and blank, stared heavenward. A stream of blood flowed from his mouth. The head rolled and sank back below the surface of the brown and red water.

The commotion overhead, perhaps mercifully, served as a distraction. Chester and I didn't have time to ponder the significance of seeing our first death.

The Rebels set fire to the bridge and withdrew to the west through town with wagons in tow. There appeared to be hostages inside. A small Union cavalry unit gave chase on the north side of the river as other Yankees negotiated the flaming bridge.

Another skirmish erupted somewhere in the direction of my farm. The sounds of battle gave way to the crackling and roaring of the inferno hovering over our heads.

Chester and I moved upriver a few dozen paces and stood there, helpless, and watched the fire devour the bridge. Fire blasted out of the bridge's two windows, licking the roof. Embers floated down on us as sections collapsed. We backed up a hundred yards to escape the heat. The timbers groaned and cracked until the whole thing fell into the dark water with a crash and a monstrous hiss.

When the fighting on the street above us died down, we followed the bank toward home. As we squished through the mud, something ahead and to the left caught my eye. We slowed our approached. A wounded Johnny Reb had apparently fallen off the road and rolled into the vegetation on the embankment. He didn't appear to be moving.

I got within arm's length. His chest was slowly rising and falling. A large crimson stain was growing outward through the fabric of his jeans-cloth coat. His shimmering eyes held a look of horror and were fixed on mine. A tear carved a path through the grime on his face. His chest stopped expanding. His face relaxed and almost appeared peaceful. He became still.

Dumbfounded, Chester and I stared, watching for his chest to move again, expecting him to wake up from a nap or give up on his game of playing dead. I stared at the brass buttons on his breast. They didn't move.

His vacant eyes were fixed upward like the soldier who almost fell on me. It was as if he were engaged in a staring contest with God. The sound of gunfire faded toward the west as a minute of stillness passed between Chester, the body, and me. Chester crossed his arms, hugging himself, a strange, vacant expression on his face. We stared silently, taking in the gravity of the situation in which we had found ourselves. My stomach crawled. A cold sweat ran between my shoulder blades.

"Come on, Vit," Chester said as he grabbed my sleeve. "We've got to get outta here." His eyes turned downward. He shook his head slowly as he walked away. Tearing my eyes from the fallen soldier, I followed Chester. Yards from the dead soldier, an unseen force prodded us into a sprint. We suddenly couldn't be far enough away from the body. We fled to the McEwen house to report to the Colonel.

As we crossed the yard, Mammy poked her head out of the smoke house.

"Boys! Come sees me a minute."

We hopped inside, the smell of soot and cooked meat flooding my nose. She drove a cleaver into the cutting board and wiped sweat from her brow with the back of her sleeve.

"Tell me boys," an enthusiastic grin on her face, "what's all da commotion bout? And don't leave out no particulars." I gave her a summary of what had transpired, her eyes bulging with excitement. She wiped her hands on her apron. "Ya'll done good, boys. Real good. Now run along inside."

We started out the door when she reminded us, "Now, keep this to yo selves, ya hear?"

The Colonel met us in the parlor. He stabbed a finger in my chest while barking reproach, his breath smelling like moth balls. "How many times do I have to tell you two to cut out all the skylarkin'? What do you think you're doing carrying on like that when there's a battle afoot?" He said it as if he'd wanted everyone in the house to hear. "You'll get yourself killed!" We bowed our heads.

"Get in my library!"

"Yes, sir."

Closing the doors on the rest of the household, he had us sit down. At his desk, he pulled paper and pen from the drawer.

"How did this happen?" the Colonel said through

gritted teeth. Before we could answer he started again, "Did you boys scout the northern approaches this morning?"

"No sir," I said. "We were here doing our lessons. I think Lillian and Annie were supposed to be on that side. Besides, sir, I don't think we could have prevented that one. The Rebels came in so fast. It was a skilled cavalry unit."

"Okay, okay. You're probably right. Tell me what you saw."

"The Rebels burned the bridge," I said. The Colonel's face remained firm.

"Go on."

I looked at Chester. He was eating his own lips.

"There was around three hundred Union soldiers," I said. "A foraging party I guess. The Rebels captured close to twenty Yankees. Looked like one major, two captains, and I think a lieutenant."

The Colonel stood and gave us each a pat on the head and walked over to the window. For a moment, he stared into the yard as if in deep thought. I grabbed the folding knife off his desk and played with it out of his line of sight. It had a smooth, bone handle that cradled the knife blade. I enjoyed the way it felt in my hand.

"I need to ask you two boys to take on a little more if you're willing."

"Yes, sir?" Chester said enthusiastically.

"I want the two of you to scout the whole northern approach. I'm dedicating teams two and three to the south side."

"Why, sir?" I said. "Why just the two of us alone on the north?" I flipped the knife blade out to the locked position.

"Despite what happened this morning, I believe more raids will come from the south from now on. Because of this, I want more eyes down that way. Plus, I have extra work for you two."

He took a pipe from his desk and lit it. He took a couple puffs and leaned against the bureau. I carefully closed the knife back up.

"I've heard through the grapevine the Union high command in Nashville is interested in a full-scale occupation of Franklin and that they intend to build a sizable garrison on the northern banks of the Harpeth. They'll want to guard the railroad and the Nashville pike."

"Figuer's Bluff?" I guessed.

"Yes, that's right. I want you to keep an eye on Figuer's Bluff."

"Yes, sir."

"Give me a daily account of what's going on."

"Yes, sir."

"I'm proud of you boys. That is all." He walked toward the door.

"Thank you sir," we said. I carefully snuck the knife back on to his desk.

"Oh, and keep your lips sealed. Report only to me. Don't tell Mammy anything at all."

The heat of shame flooded my cheeks.

"Remember, if the wrong people hear of our enterprise, we could be hanged for what we're doing."

Before we could reply, his eyes pinned me to the back of the chair.

"If Adelicia knows about this, what do you think she'll do, Vitus?"

"Want to join us," I said.

"That's right. And do you think I want my little girl out there doing what you all do?"

"No, sir." I shook my head.

"Then go on now."

"Yes, sir."

THE COLONEL NEVER PRESSURED US INTO OUR ROLES IN espionage. We were happy to do it and he provided more for us than our parents were able. He had been like another father to us. Ever since his fifteen-year-old son, Richard, died in '59, he and his wife Cynthia felt it was their calling to help boys like Chester and me get an education and learn how to be proper gentlemen. There was a dozen or more of us that met at his home on weekday mornings for lessons.

The McEwens were real hospitable. They'd even board city kids whose parents weren't around. But podunk kids like me didn't always have the pleasure. If I was gone too long, my folks would get sore. They expected me to help out around the farm. More often than not, Chester would stay at the McEwens on account of his father being a no good drunk.

Before our older brothers left, the four of us would meet under a squatty oak beside the pond on the Campbell property and walk together to the McEwen house. Of late, I'd run to the pond alone and wait for Chester, skipping rocks at the ducks. If he showed up, we'd walk together and talk about girls and how gross they were, that fat puppy Jimmy McKlusky and his big mouth, and espionage missions.

Chester and I had wanted to enlist too, but the Colonel wouldn't hear of it. "You're still babies," he'd say. "You just make every effort to stay out of trouble, and get educated." He flashed me a wink.

Barely in the throes of puberty, Chester and I knew more about the war than most adults in town. In addition to reading war updates in *Harper's Weekly*, short talks with Moscow Carter, and gathering intelligence through our reconnoitering, we were also privy to the latest news from the Colonel. He'd had his ear to the ground and plenty of sources to feed him information, including Chester and me. We picked up a considerable amount while hiding under the front porch listening in on hushed exchanges with visitors or cupping our ears on the library door.

We didn't learn much news from our folks. Ever since James left, my parents had almost become mutes when it came to the war. Chester's pa wasn't a fount of information either.

"The damn Yankees are vermin hellbent on snatching the freedom from our calloused, agrarian hands," he'd spit out in a drunken slur. "The goddamn Yankees want cheap cotton, and without slaves they can't get it. What do they expect us to do? It's our God-given right to own and make use of Africans."

Chester's pa never owned a slave and never would. The two of them lived in a ramshackle house just west of town in a flood plain. Even if he'd had enough land to make a decent living, he couldn't maintain a farm on account of his alcoholism. He'd had a drinking problem since I'd known him. Things only got worse after his wife died. His consumption exceeded his tolerance tenfold. The drunker he got, the more belligerent he became. Every now and again, Chester would show up at the McEwen house with a black eye. I swore, if I ever caught his father hitting him, I'd beat him to death with a hickory stick.

My folks, on the other hand, didn't believe in the idea of slavery. Of course we had a small operation that didn't require much help. Subsistence farming really only required the hands of family members to tend to it. That's all Pa wanted. Just to get by and to be left well enough alone. He thought the institution of slavery was wrong, but he had taken grievance to the trespassing and thievery of the Northerners and sought retribution.

According to conversations between Pa and Ma after they'd wrongly assumed I was asleep, Pa was of the mind to join James and the Army of Tennessee and fight off the northern aggression, but his service in the wars with the Indians had left him with an ugly limp. A limp I'd known since I was a baby. He had been struck by an arrow that shattered his femur. Hobbled and unable to escape, an Indian warrior tried scalping Pa and nearly succeeded. Pa somehow managed to avoid a full scalping. We don't know what happened to the Indian, but Pa was left with a gruesome scar on his head. He had a bald patch where his forelock should have been. The skin was a little gnarled up. He often wore a hat to cover it up.

He nearly died from the infection in his leg and scalp,

but somehow managed to make it home. He never gave any particulars of his time fighting the Indians in the west, except to voice his disapproval of us playing Find the Indian. The kids in town often asked James and me about Pa's scarred scalp. They wanted to hear the story of the soldier who survived a scalping. We usually did what we could to brush it off and change the subject. We understood it had been very traumatic so we avoided the topic and never brought up subject of Indians around Pa.

The steely determination and steady pace visible in his labored gait echoed who he was as a man. A principled man who would not give up without a fight. But fighting was not physically possible for him. Splitting firewood or plowing the fields served as his release from the frustration of his handicap.

Chester and I shared the sentiments of James and our fathers and we intended to do something to contribute to the war effort. The good thing about being a twelve-year-old boy in an enemy-occupied town is no one would suspect you as a spy.

NINE

The winter of 1862 was dreary and melancholy. Food was scarce at home and the weather was unforgiving. A group of Invaders came to our farm and stole our pigs and most of our chickens. They even took our horse, Frank. I had been out looking for ginseng root in the northern hills when they had come. I was real sore with Pa when I came home to find he had allowed the bluebellies to steal our livestock.

My brother was gone and now our animals were gone. My parents weren't much in the mood for holiday festivities, but they accompanied me to a party at the McEwen house. Normally we'd go to St. Paul's for Christmas Service, but the rector quit and joined the Army of Tennessee and the Yankees had promptly moved into the sanctuary to use as a barracks.

The McEwens invited several families to their house on Christmas Eve, but only the Carters and a few others showed up. Many had moved away.

While my parents and the McEwens exchanged pleasantries in the foyer, I stayed on the porch for a moment and stared at the scant Christmas decorations haphazardly hung from a handful of buildings and lampposts in town. Instead of friendly caroling, the crack of rifle fire drifted on the wind. Even on Christmas Eve, small skirmishes between the Rebels and Yankees were taking place nearby.

Inside, the house smelled like woodsmoke from the large, stone fireplace, cinnamon, and baked Christmas goose. Chester and I were quite pleased to see Wad Carter was in attendance. He'd had a long recovery in a hospital after Shiloh and had only recently come home. He told us of his adventure with the army. He described the battle at Shiloh as the Devil's playground. That it was a scene he hoped we'd never have to see.

"Did you see the Rebel yet?" he asked.

"The Rebel?"

"Yeah, the *Chattanooga Daily Rebel?* No, I guess you wouldn't have. I may have the only copy that's made it to Franklin."

He pulled a folded leaf of paper from his coat pocket. "Look here."

He handed me the paper, which I promptly unfolded. It was indeed a page from the *Chattanooga Daily Rebel*. I had never heard of it.

"Look here," Wad said again as he pointed at a column. A heading read, "By Grapevine and Otherwise from Middle Tennessee Camp near Murfreesboro, Nov. 20 1862."

I scanned the article. It was a colorful and detailed description of life in camp. The author told of the boring monotony of army routine then provided a literary narration of the forces of tyranny and oppression descending upon the south.

At the bottom of the article, it said, "Well I have written enough. You can read this in broken doses. With many compliments and much respect, Mint Julep, Fils."

"This is dandy, Wad," I said, handing it back to him. "But I'm not sure if I see the significance."

"That's Tod."

"Tod?"

"Mint Julep is my brother Theodrick Carter! He's become a war correspondent."

A smile stretched across my face and my heart quickened.

"You're kidding," Chester said.

"Nope. He sent this to us with a letter. Isn't this great, boys? Now we can hear all about what our brothers are up to."

"What did the letter say?" I asked.

"Mostly that he was alright and that he was writing for the Rebel. Oh, yeah, I almost forgot. He mentioned that he hooked up with George and James."

Butterflies kicked around in my stomach.

"This is a great Christmas present," I said. "I have to tell my folks."

I found Ma in the kitchen receiving cider from Mammy and told her all about it. She was excited but I think the joy was feigned. A look of worry had permanently been etched in her face.

Everyone listened to Addie play the piano while she and her sister, Frances sang carols. Green boughs of pine and spruce, and sprigs of holly with thick shiny leaves and red berries, were carefully placed on the mantel and among the china. Mayor McEwen had personally cut down a pine Christmas tree that morning. It stood in the front window, reaching to the tall ceiling, decorated with more holly, beads of dried cranberries, and small candles. All the guests had wine and ate the traditional Christmas pudding Mammy had made. I had to credit everyone for their attempt to remain festive.

After a round of applause, conversations recommenced and inevitably changed to the war and the dangers of a full-scale battle happening in our quiet village.

The rest of the kids and I sat on the floor by the fireplace most of the evening playing checkers and Blind Man's Bluff. My ears, like a dog's, rotated and tuned in to adult conversations.

"The fight this morning was too close," Billy's mom said. She was referring to a raid made by the Texas Rangers on a Union forage train near the Concord Baptist Church not far from where we stood.

"I agree," said another lady I didn't know. "We're moving to my sister's in Manchester the day after Christmas."

"Now, we hadn't decided that for sure, Sarah," her husband added.

"I think we should all leave town before blood is spilled on our very streets," she returned. The party went from bad to worse. Everyone fell silent.

"Well," my pa said as he raised a glass. "Merry Christmas."

. . .

THE CHRISTMAS TREE AT OUR HOUSE PALED IN COMPARISON TO the McEwens. I had helped Pa cut down a sorry little cedar tree on a hill behind our back field. Our decorations were limited to holly berries and small trinkets James and I had made as kids. I swept the hearth and Pa built a fire. Ma concocted her special eggnog and gave me a small glass. She asked Pa to read passages of the Bible out loud. Pa wasn't a good reader, but he had memorized enough verses to feign reading from the pages.

Afterward, we held hands as Ma prayed to God to watch over James. Afterward, the three of us sat together in the warmth of the fire. Ma crocheted while I read aloud to them. Ma said my reading filled the silence and occupied her mind. I lay on the floor, with my book propped against the hearth, and read about Daniel Boone passing through the Cumberland Gap to the promised land of Kentucky, and when he first came upon the sprawling blue grass.

The absence of James weighed heavily on us.

Christmas morning, I spent some quality time with Pa digging through the frosted earth to make a new hole for the outhouse. Without Frank, we had to push the outhouse over to the new hole ourselves. Pa was gracious enough to let me fill in the old sludge hole myself. "Merry Christmas," I told him sarcastically. Through a cloud of my misting breath, I watched the back of him as he wordlessly retreated to the house.

EVEN ON CHRISTMAS DAY AND THE DAY AFTER, MORE skirmishes took place near Franklin. News came in mid-

January of a large battle in Murfreesboro that cost around ten thousand Confederate and thirteen thousand Union casualties. It was hard to deny that the scope and close proximity of the war was more serious than anyone had imagined. Ma was beside herself with worry about James.

Franklin had become a foreign town. There were Yankees at the barber, Yankees at the drug store, Yankees on the corners and in our churches. Some were ornery and some were jovial. One played chase with a few boys in the square, as if they were his own. Did he have a family up north?

It was growing more and more difficult to carry on like normal citizens with Invaders keeping a watchful eye on us. Conversations between neighbors turned to whispers when one approached. Rumors of an impending battle circulated and secret meetings to discuss preparations replaced casual conversations at the poker table.

CHESTER AND I CONTINUED TO KEEP AN EYE ON THE Invaders. Hiding along the wooded banks of the Harpeth, we watched them place pontoons in the river to serve as a temporary bridge to Nashville. From the roof of Hiram Mason Lodge, the tallest building in town, we studied the construction progress on top of Figuer's Bluff. They'd cut down trees and torn apart fences for nearly a mile in every direction and dragged them to the top of the bluff, sixty feet above the river. They dismantled the Harpeth Male Academy and carted bricks to the building site that loomed over the town.

In late winter, we scaled the steep escarpment separating the river from the top of Figuer's Bluff. From the foot of the fort's earthen walls, a commanding view of Franklin spread out below us as far as Winstead Hill to the south and the City Cemetery to the west. Many of the larger trees in and around town had been cut down to provide a clear view of the roads, yards, and fields.

In the twilight hours, while the Invaders built bonfires and drank their booze, we snuck around for a better look at the interior of the fort. From the shadows of boulders and tree stumps, we memorized everything we saw.

IN THE COLONEL'S LIBRARY, WHILE THE OTHERS WERE studying arithmetic in the kitchen, Chester and I gave a full report.

"Did anyone clap eyes on you today?" the Colonel asked.

"No, sir. Not as far as we could tell. Right, Chester?"

He shrugged his shoulders in agreement.

"So tell me everything."

"Well, sir," I started, "they're still digging and piling dirt for the ramparts and fortifying them with timber. There are three main walls. One along the bluff and the other two making a triangle. The trenches are a good ten feet deep and around sixteen feet wide. The parapets on top are another six or eight feet tall."

The Colonel nodded his head as he took notes.

"My best guess is the wall overlooking the Harpeth is better than two hundred yards long. The other two are about half that, each. The northern and eastern walls are fortified."

"What's going on inside the walls?" the Colonel interrupted.

"Well, there's also a long blast wall, they made with all the bricks from the academy," Chester added.

"Yeah, that's right," I said. "In the middle, there's the basement of an old house, where it looks like they're building a powder magazine."

"Anything else?" The Colonel dipped his pen in ink with anticipation.

"Yes, sir. Lot's more."

"Shoot, then."

"It looks like there's a cistern that will hold lots and lots of water."

"Mmkay." He chewed his tongue and scratched at his paper.

"Can I go back to talking about the outside of the fort?" I asked, anxious to get everything out while I still remembered it all.

"Well, yeah. Of Course."

"Well, I counted thirty-five cannon emplacements on the tops of the walls." I looked at Chester. "Thirty-five, right?"

"Yeah."

"Are there thirty-five cannons up there?" The Colonel said with a look of concern on his face.

"Well, sir, there are two thirty-pound siege cannons, five field guns already set up, and another eight waiting to be placed. So fifteen pieces of artillery in total so far, sir."

"There's also a bunch of rifle pits just outside of the walls on the Harpeth side," Chester added.

"Excellent work, boys! I would imagine that's all you have for me." He pushed back his desk chair.

"No, sir," I said. The Colonel sat back down with a smile.

"Okay, let me have it."

"Well, sir, as you may already know, General Gordon Granger is overseeing the fort's construction." The Colonel nodded. "And his chief engineer is Captain W. E. Merrill."

"Anything else?"

"Just one question sir," I said as I eyeballed his bookshelves.

"Boys, you could ask just about anything you want. You two have done some mighty fine work." He stood and walked around the desk behind our chairs.

"Can I borrow another book?" I asked sheepishly.

"Vitus Swinggate," he said loudly as he smacked the back of my shoulder, "you can borrow whatever you want."

I headed toward the bookshelves.

The Colonel had always encouraged me to read. One morning a few years back, he'd caught me covetously running my fingertips across the spines of the collection in his library.

"You can take one or two home with you as long as you return them," he'd said from the doorway. Hands clasped behind his back, he stepped toward me.

"You have a knack for reading and writing, Vitus Swinggate. If you choose to, you could use your gift to know the world around you and explore the world beyond you. You've been dealt a tough hand, but education can be your ticket out when this war's over."

I gladly accepted his offer and borrowed books one at a time and took them home to the farm. As soon as I'd finish feeding the chickens and goats and cleaning out the coop or barn, I'd scurry into the hayloft of Pa's dilapidated barn to read. I loved science, particularly birds and plants. And I enjoyed works like Emerson's *Self Reliance*, Thoreau's *Walden*, and Franklin's *Poor Richard's Almanac*. Since the Invaders stole our pigs along with Frank I'd had more time to read.

"Oh, here's some more reading material." He pulled a piece of paper from a desk drawer. "It's the latest from Mint Julep about the battle in Murfreesboro. Nothing about James or George. Sorry."

I took the copy of the *Chattanooga Daily Rebel* from him and scanned over the print.

"After you pick out a book," the Colonel said as he sat down at his desk, "get yourselves some gingerbread and join the others. Mammy just made it fresh."

"Yes, sir."

Taking advantage of his good humor, I grabbed one of his newest books, *On The Origin of Species*, by a fella named Charles Darwin.

Envy glared like a hot fire from Jimmy McKlusky and one of his cronies, Roger, as we closed the library door behind us. They knew we were up to something, but not sure what. Either way, Jimmy craved the attention Chester and I received from the Colonel.

Chester went off to play with Addie's little sister, Frances in the yard while I found my favorite tree on the

McEwen property. The black oak was of large circumference and forked low to the ground, making many wide elbows to choose from. I climbed up and settled into one, anxious to read what Mint Julep had to report.

My entire body clenched as I took in his detailed report of the carnage he witnessed. I feared for James as Tod described the scene around Murfreesboro as a bloody carnival, fiery tempest, galling fire, and a bloody banquet. One hundred and thirty-four of the four hundred men of the 20th Tennessee had become casualties in the fight.

Tod, having been well educated as a lawyer, authored a good tale. His writing was graphic, illustrative, and scholarly. A work that rivaled many of the great pieces of literature in the McEwen library. The chronicle was tiresome to read for all its intensity. In the end, he wrote that the demons of hell seemed to have met in wild, blood-drunken revelry and the Rebels finally drove the Invaders away, howling through woods and fields.

He concludes the correspondence simply, "Well good day, I must close. MINT JULEP."

Upon folding the paper into fours, I felt all the muscles in my lower abdomen release all the tension the letter had built. Tod's illustration of battle struck a visceral fear in me.

TEN

A clap of thunder sent convulsions through me, shaking my fishing pole and jiggling the line, making tiny ripples in the water. A cloud of doves took flight in a humming, complaining mass and flew across the river away from town. A smaller rumbled followed seconds later. The sky was bright blue. Not a cloud to be seen. *Not thunder.* Gooseflesh surfaced on my arms as the concussion bounced through the surrounding hills.

The incredulous look on Chester's face mirrored mine.

"Was that what I think it was, Vitus?"

The past few weeks, the Yankees in Fort Granger had been firing artillery into the fields on the southeast of town gauging range and honing accuracy. Small craters peppered the pastures, sometimes only a few paces from where children played tag. Cannon balls hitting dirt and grass made an unearthly thud as they dug into the ground. This new concussion was different somehow.

Chester threw his pole in the mud beside the water's edge and took off. I chased him up the riverbank, slipping on rocks, grabbing tree roots. Reaching the top of the embankment, we dove to the ground, slithered to level ground, and carefully poked our heads above the grass to have a look toward town center.

A small field of early switchgrass separated us from the city cemetery. Recently neglected tombs and headstones peeked out of untended grass between Indigo Street and West Margin. Beyond the cemetery a spattering of houses surrounded the buildings and church steeples situated around the square. Figuer's Bluff was to our left, looming above the peak of Hiram Masonic Lodge. A crow cawed a warning.

Another thunderclap, like a punch in the chest. We flinched and instinctively buried our heads in our arms. The smell of mud was somehow comforting. In front of me, a tuft of clover dangled over a small shelf of mud. For a fleeting moment I found myself looking for one with four leaves.

"That was definitely cannon fire," I whispered. Chester nodded agreement. We poked our heads back up like groundhogs. We weren't able to see the source of the blasts, but we knew full well where it had come from.

This time the blasts were deeper, more powerful than the ones they'd been shooting into the fields.

"That was no ordinary cannon," Chester said. "That had to be a siege gun from the fort."

He was right. And somehow the blasts felt more significant. Ominous.

"Let's go!" I said.

We both scrambled to our feet and ran across the field and through the cemetery dodging headstones and monuments. We dropped down behind a box-like tomb to catch our breath. The faint sound of rifle fire carried on the wind from the south.

The tomb's lid was slightly ajar, a stale, heavy air escaping from inside. I noticed the engraving on top. "Sacred in the MEMORY OF Colonel Guilford Dudley," was etched in the stone. Below that it read, "Virginia, April 17, 1756 departed this life the 3 of Feb 1833."

An original Rebel. A revolutionary Rebel. It was a week from his birthday. *Happy early birthday, pard.*

The streets were strangely empty. It looked safe to continue toward the action. We looked at each other, nodded, and sprung over the tomb and darted across North Margin Street. Our backs slammed into the side of a small house, the clapboards giving slightly to the impact.

We both jumped at the sound of another blast. "That surely came from the fort," Chester said.

"I think they're shootin' toward Lewisburg Pike. Let's get to the McEwen house."

Chester looked around the corner of the house and started off toward the larger, brick houses on Bridge Street. I was right on his heels.

We were so worked up, we barely paused before turning the corner and running up the middle of Bridge Street. Smaller blasts came from the direction of Lewisburg Pike.

"There's return fire!" Chester yelled.

Rifle fire grew in volume and frequency, popping like green pine in flames.

When we saw it was all clear, we shot across West Margin Street. The concussion of another cannon fire nearly knocked me off my feet and successfully flung Chester to the ground. He practically bounced back off the hard-packed dirt and caught up with me.

The McEwen house was intact and seemingly quiet. "Let's take to the roof," I said.

"Why ain't we goin' inside and watch from a winda? Colonel won't mind."

"They're all probably hidin' in the cellar. If they hear us come in, they'll make us hide too."

"Ahh, gotcha."

We ran past the meat house and snuck onto the back porch and peered in through a window. No movement.

Standing on the porch railing, I boosted Chester over the lip of the roof and he pulled me up after him. We slunk across the flat roof to the windows. After confirming we hadn't been heard, we shimmied up a drain pipe to the highest section of the house, skittered across the ridge, and crouched together near one of the chimneys like two turkey vultures waiting for a meal to fall dead in the vicinity.

From General Granger's fort on Figuer's Bluff on our left, to the roof of the Carter house stabbing up from a naked hillside on our right, the only obstruction of our view was the bell tower of St. Paul's.

There was definitely a battle afoot. White plumes of smoke floated on the breeze over the Lewisburg Pike. Rifles cracked back and forth in the direction of Douglas Church.

Eyes fixed toward the south, we jumped at the sound of scraping and clunking behind us.

"Someone's fixin' to come up here," Chester whispered. We lowered to our chests and slid behind the peak of the roof on the opposite slope. My heart pounded against the shingles.

"I seen you idjits already," came a voice, clearly recognizable. I popped my head over the peak to confirm. Standing on the roof of the porch wearing a goofy smile, was Jimmy McKlusky. He had climbed out the upstairs window. His thick head was covered in what looked like a pile of dead pine needles and his face was covered with matching freckles. He was hard to look at.

"Shut up, fathead," I whisper-yelled. "You're gonna get us caught. Go away!"

"What y'all doin up there?"

"None of your consarn business!"

"I want to see." He pulled at the shingles and gutter, making all kinds of racket.

"If you don't shut up, I'll beat the tar out of you like the last twenty-five times I did." My hands curled into fists.

"Your little girlfriend would get sore at ya again if ya did."

"She's not my girlfriend, butt sniffer!"

"Might as well help his fat butt," Chester suggested. "He ain't gonna give up til' he's up here and he's sure as shootn' gonna alert the entire household of his attempt."

I rolled my eyes and let out a huff. "Come on."

McKlusky was as heavy as he was ugly. How he'd gotten so thick would forever be a mystery since most kids running around Franklin were half-starved. He and his bigger brother, Bubba, were unusually larger than most kids, but that didn't keep me from pounding both of them. The McKlusky boys were the official town bullies. They were persistent and dumb as ticks. I knew this first hand because I'd given both of them enough lickings for a lifetime, but they continued to annoy me.

Jimmy McKlusky's favorite subject of torment was Addie and whether she and I were an item. This was poppycock and I usually finished heated discussions with flying fists. He was always asking for it. And every time he made what I considered a request for a beating, I'd gladly given it to him. Unfortunately for McKlusky, my affinity for fisticuffs exceeded his capacity for bullying.

Even his older brother, Bubba had once challenged me to a boxing match on a gravel bar in the Harpeth. I don't know where I got it, but I was a natural pugilist. Though much larger than me, Bubba didn't have a chance. I peppered his face with punches before he surmised what was happening to him. I had to pull him out of the river afterward so he wouldn't drown.

Addie, standing on the bank in her pale yellow Sunday dress and bare feet, watched the whole thing transpire. She did not much care for such crass behavior. As I dropped the wet mass that was Bubba on the gravel, a slight smile of approval cautiously made itself known on her otherwise horror-stricken face.

She was not my girlfriend. What good is a girl to a twelve-year-old boy? I didn't have time for that kind of nonsense. Last summer she gave me my first peck on the cheek after I'd shoved McKlusky into the rose bushes for calling her a whooperup when she was singing "Amazing Grace" from her porch swing. I had to admit, I didn't hate it when she did it. But she was not my girlfriend.

AFTER TRYING TO HAUL THE LARD BUTT UP TO NO AVAIL, I told McKlusky he had to stay on the porch roof until he implemented a new routine of diet and exercise that would shed some weight. Without a word, he slid around the corner of the porch roof and made his way to the front of the house. Chester and I floated back across the roof to our lookout point.

I happened to be looking to the northeast when a puff of smoke emanated from the fort on the hill. A second later, a teeth-chattering boom echoed through the air. Almost immediately after, there was a report to the south in the direction of the O'Moore House. It sounded like an explosion mixed with brick crumbling.

"Balls!" McKlusky screamed from below us. "Those are siege guns firin' from Fort Granger! What in hell is goin' on?"

Neither Chester nor I replied. We were more interested in the sight of hundreds of Rebel cavalry charging over the hill into town from the south attacking an entrenchment of Yankees. Mouths agape, the three of us stared in wonder as the two forces collided. I felt myself shiver as a chill ran over my skin, giving me gooseflesh.

Columns of Rebels from the south filed up Lewisburg and Columbia Pike toward earthworks the Federals had constructed along the Carter Property. When the troops on Columbia approached the Carter property, Granger's siege guns lobbed shells on them. Blooms of soil and grass left craters in yards and gardens. One explosion dismounted a Confederate soldier, throwing his rifle into the grass. He pulled himself along the ground until he disappeared under a clump of brush. The horse, panicking, ran between houses in the direction of town square.

The huge guns swiveled and shelled the forces near Douglas Church. The Rebels responded in kind with field cannons, but to little effect. For hours the battle carried on and on. The cacophony bouncing our heads around and thumping our chests.

The Rebels nearly pushed the Invaders back to the fort, but after a short fight, they had been repelled back to the south. The staccato of gunfire gradually abated to intermittent cracks from rifles. Then there was a still silence. Not just in the air but finally in my chest.

Heavy smoke and dust blanketed Franklin. A thick, noxious fog bank rolled over the town, consuming every structure. It swallowed St. Paul's before gobbling us up. It coated my skin and choked my lungs. All three of us erupted in coughing fits.

"We better git," I said to Chester, my voice faltering from intruding dust and fear.

We felt our way across the roof. It was slow-going, but we eventually found the drain pipe.

"Adelicia!" A deep voice penetrated the smothering quiet. It was the Colonel. It sounded like he was on the side porch. "Addie, get back in here!"

I stopped half way down the pipe, ears ringing.

"But I want to see if the boys are okay, Pa," she yelled from the porch below us.

We froze. Chester above me was a silhouette, a friendly gargoyle looking over the house. McKlusky had made it around the corner and I was close enough to see he held a special kind of fear in his eyes. It had just dawned on him that the Colonel would flip his lid if he knew we were on his roof.

"Get back in the basement this instant, Adelicia McEwen!"

"Yes, sir."

Don't tell him we're up here, a voice inside me begged.

"Should we go home, or go inside?" Chester asked after the clack of the door. It was a good question. On the one hand, if we went in, he'd want to know why we would do such a fathead thing like watching the battle from his roof. On the other hand, if we went home, we'd have to navigate the menacing fog.

"I might live to regret it," I said, "but let's just stay here. It'd be a lot easier. But don't tell the Colonel we were on his roof. Okay?"

"Yeah."

"Okay, McKlusky? You hear me? Don't go tattlin' on us or I'll give you an anointing you won't soon forget." I shook my fist, barely visible in the murk.

"Mmkay."

"Close that window and come down with us," I said a little louder than I meant to. "You'll get busted if you go back in that way." McKlusky closed it loudly.

"Well, let's go face the music."

We slowly made it over the roof, onto the porch railing, then to the security of the porch planks. The world around us was still gray and thick.

I walked ahead of them toward the door. It was unlocked as usual.

ELEVEN

The entire household was still holed up in the cellar. The three of us slowly descended the stairs to our impending chastising from the Colonel.

Mrs. McEwen and her four daughters stared at us, a mixture of fear and vexation on their faces. The yellow glow of a candle highlighted the soft features of Addie's face. Her dark hair, in a loose ponytail, covered her ears and lay softly on her cotton nightshirt.

"Tarnation, boys!" The Colonel started in on us. "Mind explaining what on earth you thought you were doing out there?"

My face burned with embarrassment. Addie turned her eyes toward the floor. And for that, I was grateful.

Chester was first to speak up. "We was fishin'…and when they started shootin', we hid."

"Were," the Colonel said.

"Sir?"

"You *were* fishing," he corrected.

"Sir, we thought it would be safer to hide—"

"That dog won't hunt with me, boy. I know what you were up to. I could hear you on my roof. And during a battle? Don't that beat all."

Lamp light sparkled on the spittle gathering on his white beard. "Your mother must be worried sick about you, Vitus Swinggate. You know she's beside herself with worry about James already. You want to give her a complete come-apart?"

I shook my head.

He looked at Chester. "No offense, son, but I doubt your pa has the wherewithal to give a tinker's damn where you are. I'm sure he's passed out with a bottle of bug juice on his chest. Either way, you two had better skedaddle home at first light, you hear?"

"Yes, sir."

"Sir," McKlusky piped up, "I heard them on the roof and was just outside to call them—"

"Balderdash, Jimmy! You're just as guilty."

"Yes, sir. Sorry, sir."

"All y'all get out of my sight, but don't you leave this house 'til morning."

Later, the Colonel asked me to come upstairs and have a look around with him. We didn't do much looking, he wanted to know what I had seen from the roof. So I told him.

AFTER A QUIET HOUR PASSED, THE COLONEL TOOK THE KIDS outside to have a look around. It was still foggy and smelled strange. He instructed us to look for any weapons that might have been left behind, but not to go beyond St. Paul's. It was like an Easter egg hunt only we were searching for dead bodies and war materiel.

We came across the body of a Confederate soldier beside Fair Street, a gaping hole in his neck. The girls screamed and ran for the house. The curious boys stood over him and stared until the Colonel found us.

"Someone will be by to pick him up later, I'm sure." His voice was somber.

"Vitus, grab his sidearm."

A Colt Army Model revolver was lying beside him. The weight of it was more significant than I'd anticipated—its metal cold and hard. I handed it to the Colonel. McKlusky huffed and walked toward the house. Everyone else tore their eyes from the dead man and followed.

AFTER SUPPER, MAMMY SET UP BED ROLLS FOR US ON THE floor in the corner that we employed as mattresses. The moment I closed my eyes, gunfire and cannon blasts rattled in my head. Men falling and cavalrymen charging, mouths gaping, Rebel yells spewing. The man crawling into the bushes, his rifle lying in the clover.

Where is my brother, I thought. After witnessing a battle from afar, I couldn't imagine what it was like for him.

Sleep would not come that night.

· · ·

What must have been just before sunrise, I gave up the idea of sleeping and snuck out of the house into the lonely dark. It looked as if a storm cloud had descended on the town and had no plans to move.

The air was still heavy and thick with smoke and mist. Visibility was nearly zero. The fog still had a peculiar smell to it, not one I readily recognized. Perhaps the smell of gunpowder mixed with despair.

The silence was deafening. It was like a ghost town. A quiet chirp from a cricket penetrated the stillness from the corner of the yard. Then silence again.

I worked my way through the front lawn onto Fair Street, and slowly walked in the direction where the man had fallen in the bushes. It was beyond St. Paul's so I hadn't been able to investigate earlier.

After a painstaking search, I felt a rifle in the clover. I pointed it as if ready to fire. It felt heavy and powerful, the barrel exceedingly long. It was a Whitworth, a rare find. I had seen them in *Harper's Weekly*. Queen Victoria had shot one from a special mount. A handful of these rifles made it to the Confederate army and were used by sharpshooters for long range shots. The man I presumed was still lying in the bushes, must have been a skilled marksman.

Whitworth in hand, I crawled toward the bushes the soldier had squirmed under. Apprehensively, I felt my way around in the dark until I found him, stiff and cold like a life-sized doll made of wood. After shaking off a wave of repulsion, I ran my hand over his dirty uniform and rigid body. Once I found his cartridge pouch I slithered out of the bushes, glad to be away from the corpse. I stood and slung the rifle over my shoulder by the strap. I pushed away thoughts worming their way into my head of James lying like a stiff doll on a battlefield somewhere.

I quickly snuck back toward the McEwen house. The swishing of my feet through the grass was interrupted by a faint clomp, clomp, clomp to my right. I changed direction and headed toward the front of St. Paul's. A muffled whinny. A horse. The hoof beats were erratic. A couple clomps here, a couple there. It definitely didn't sound like anyone was riding it.

I crept toward the noise. I found the horse chewing on a bush in the church courtyard. I approached him slowly, whispering so as not to startle him. He gave me a greeting nicker. I talked to him in my most unexcitable tone until I was within arms-length.

He was beautiful. From the pale light of a nearby lamp, I could only make out a white lightning bolt blaze stretching from the top of his head to his nose. I recognized it as the horse the man with the birthmark had been abusing.

He was a magnificent bay with a shiny, black mane. Still saddled. He winced a little when I laid my palm on his neck but didn't withdraw. He seemed to welcome the company. After a minute of talking and stroking, I grabbed the saddle horn and threw myself on top.

We walked across the road and through the field around the McEwen house where we picked our way toward home. The haze thinned as the town behind us dissolved. A dim, red light filtered through miasma from the east as we found Pa's barn.

Inside, I lit a lantern and prepared a stall for my new friend. With him secure, I climbed into the loft above him and hid the Whitworth under a pile of straw. I curled up beside it and contemplated a name for the horse. I could only review a handful of contenders before I fell asleep.

A GRUNT STARTED ME AWAKE. SLOBBER, ACTING AS A BONDING agent, held straw to my cheek. I plucked two pieces off and rubbed the sleep from my eyes. Down in the stall, the horse looked at me apprehensively. He was a beautiful specimen. His body was a dark reddish brown and his mane, tail, and legs were black. The lightning bolt blaze seemed to glow.

I removed the saddle and gave him a good brushing. "Thoreau," I said out loud when the name for him popped in my head.

His flank was riddled with scars and several fresh wounds from the spurs of his abusive owner. The image of the man with the birthmark invaded my head. "I stole his horse?" I said aloud. A chill of fear ran down my spine and my lips curled slightly upward.

"He probably died in the battle," I rationalized to myself. "I'm not a horse thief, just an opportunist."

My new friend nudged me with his nose, as if to reassure me of my decision.

"I'm going for breakfast, Thoreau. You're safe now. I'll be back in a bit to check on you."

I had snuck in through the kitchen door and was chewing on a stale chunk of bread when Ma and Pa came in.

"Vitus Swinggate!" Ma glided swiftly across the floor and smacked my left cheek, almost knocking hair off my head, and immediately threw her arms around me, crying.

"Where in God's name have you been? Don't you know what's going on in town?"

"Yes, ma'am." My cheek burned, but her embrace felt warm and safe.

I told them what I had been doing as Pa leaned against the door jamb, arms crossed in front of his suspenders.

"Well, you ain't going to the McEwen House or town for that matter until this war is done," he said.

"But what about my education?" My face grew hot and tears burned behind my lids.

The expression on his face remained hard and immovable. "It's gonna have to wait. We need to concentrate on surviving here. And I don't need your mother having no more conniption fits wonderin' where you're at. You're not to leave this property again until the bluebellies leave our town. You understand, boy?"

"Yes, sir."

Ma had sat in a chair staring at the floor. She knew it would kill me to be confined to the farm by myself.

"Maybe he can still hunt to the west," she suggested as she turned teary eyes toward Pa. "And Chester can come over every now and again to play."

"As long as he stays on this side of the river,' Pa said. "And as long as Chester is handy with the chores."

Pa turned and left. He reminded me every chance he could get to stay on this side of West Harpeth. Beyond it was a high ridge, Backbone Ridge, the most prominent in county. "Indians are to the west of that ridge," he'd tell me. "I don't need to tell you how savage they are."

It could have been worse, I suppose. I guess no one really knew how to punish a child who stayed out all night during a military skirmish. Staying away from the McEwen house was a lot to ask, but with Thoreau here now, it would be a bit easier.

Quickly changing the subject, I stood and moved toward the door.

"Ma, I have something to show you." She looked up at me. Her face wrinkled with worry.

"It's nothing bad, come on." I took her hand and opened the back door. "Come on. Come look." Skepticism etched in her face, she reluctantly followed me to the barn where I introduced her to Thoreau.

"Well, what do you think?"

"Uh, what the heck, Vitus?" The words stumbled out. "Where'd he come from?"

I told her the story. I didn't tell her about the rifle I'd pilfered off the dead soldier.

"… and I figured since we had Frank stolen from us, it was only fair that we get one in return."

Ma wasn't sure how she felt about it, but she didn't seem mad. Indifferent, maybe. She patted Thoreau on the neck with a smile. "Are you going to tell Pa, or am I?"

She said no more and walked back to the house. I stayed behind to brush Thoreau.

THAT AFTERNOON, I WAS SCOOPING CHICKEN TURDS OUT OF the coop when Chester and McKlusky came crashing through the weeds. It was only upon a second glance that I noticed Addie was picking her way through the briars behind them, holding her dress up to avoid snags. My heart fluttered a little as if I were in danger or excited. I couldn't quite tell why I felt that way.

"Hey, Vit," Chester said in an upbeat voice. "Where'd you get off to last night?"

"Couldn't sleep. What'd you bring this fathead for?" I pointed my shovel load of turds at McKlusky before throwing it in the wheelbarrow.

"I don't know. He just followed me."

"Can't mind your own business, can you, McKlusky?" I said. "Well, never mind, take a look at what I found." I yanked my head toward the barn.

He and McKlusky ran inside.

"Sorry about Father yellin' at you last night," Addie said, keeping her distance from the poop. My stomach turned. "He's just worried about you boys, that's all."

"I know. It was dumb to do what we did."

A muffled "Whoa!" floated from the barn. Chester had found Thoreau in his stall. He came running out with a wide smile. "Where'd you get him?"

"He was at St. Paul's lookin' for Jesus, I spose," I said. "Brought him home last night. He's mine now."

"You should take it back," McKlusky said with a hint of jealousy, kicking up dust as he emerged from the barn.

"You should shut your bone box, before I break it," I returned.

"Well, I'll tell the Colonel you have it then." Condescension was all over McKlusky's chubby face.

"If you do, I'll clobber you for sure," I said balling up my hands. "I should hit you right now for selling us out to the Colonel last night, you no good double-crosser."

"I was just looking out for myself, that's all."

As hard as I tried to be a gentleman in front of Addie, McKlusky made my skin boil. The smug look on his face was like billows on my burning temper.

"Do your folks even know you have it? Maybe, I should go check with them."

That was it! I grabbed a handful of chicken turds and threw them at his face, two of them finding their mark next to his left eye. As he reeled, I skipped in and sunk the sole of my boot into his midsection and followed with a punch right on the chicken poop around his eye. A cloud of dirt enveloped him as he hit the ground.

"Vitus!" Addie squeaked. I felt embarrassed at my lack of self-control. I slammed the coop door and walked off into the field where I sat in the warm soil and waited for them to leave.

A few minutes later, Chester sat beside me. "They're gone. He deserved it, Vit."

"Thanks."

"Can we take him for a ride? Thoreau, I mean?"

A smile stretched across my face.

TWELVE

Pa obviously found out about Thoreau, but he never said much about it. It was as if he was trying to convince himself that the horse had been ours all along and that talking about it might somehow change that.

I rode Thoreau every day I could. I took him along the boundaries of my territory. Along the banks of the West Harpeth, my western boundary. From the east side of the river, I could see the dark ridgeline of Backbone Ridge. The allure of exploring beyond those hills pulled strongly at me. Pa made it painted it out to be wild and dangerous. A place where no white man belonged. To me it was my Cumberland Gap. I promised myself I'd find a way over that ridge like Daniel Boone did into Kentucky. I would someday set off on an expedition to explore and hunt in the uncharted territory to the west.

Thoreau and I wandered the hills in the south, and lay about in his favorite spot, the Indian burial mound near the westerly road. No one farmed around it, leaving lush grasses for him to munch on while I ran up and down the house-sized mound.

We galloped through the empty fields and took water breaks at the river. He'd drink as I jumped from tree limbs into the emerald green swimming hole.

I'd lie on the gravel bank and watch mockingbirds flitter in the branches above Thoreau as he pulled at the leaves. He'd just stand there untethered and wait for me to get my fill of daydreaming and skipping stones.

Some days, near dusk, we'd come upon white tail deer in the fields. I was always surprised how close we could get to them if I'd lay on Thoreau's back.

An idea came upon me one late afternoon when I was hunting squirrels with Pa's little rifle. To heck with squirrels, I thought. I ran home and grabbed my Whitworth rifle I had hidden in the loft.

Clutching the rifle, I climbed onto Thoreau, and headed for the back fields where I practiced loading it and shooting targets. When I felt proficient, I took Thoreau on a hunting trip. When I finally spotted a buck standing flank deep in briars, I hugged Thoreau's sweaty neck and slowed our gait. As we approached, the buck looked up at us warily, but eventually returned to rooting around. When I got within sixty yards or so, I sat up and fired.

The buck's back end crumpled but quickly rebounded into a panicked sprint. I had hit him, but missed the vitals. Thoreau and I chased him until he fell and disappeared into the vegetation. He writhed in the grass as I reloaded the rifle. I fired again into his head, quieting him forever.

I got quite a rush out of the whole ordeal. My blood

surged. Chest pounded. Instead of feeling guilty as I had thought I would, l felt elated. A sense of accomplishment.

I made a quick trip back to the barn for some rope and a knife. I field dressed the deer, thinking of the many times Pa and I had done it together in the past. Thoreau and I carried the deer back in the dark.

After my inaugural horseback hunt, I made it a point to practice my new hunting art. I didn't want to make any more deer suffer from a bad shot. I'd ride Thoreau around the farm shooting from his back at tree stumps and any small animal worth eating. I'd pretend I was on a cavalry charge shooting the enemy quail and turkey. Over time I became quite a marksmen.

Ma and Pa were always thrilled when I bagged a deer. They never questioned the implement I used to bring them down. A good buck fed us for weeks. We'd eat our share of fresh meat, and Ma would salt or dry the rest. We'd have jerky to spare. The only time I was allowed off the farm, was when Ma gave me permission to take some meat to Chester and his pa. They were both mighty grateful.

The faint sound of my name made it to my ears through the switch grass I was laying in one afternoon. I decided to ignore it. A redwing blackbird, perched on a tall wheat stalk, swung back and forth in the wind. I wondered how long he'd hang on. Overhead a large hawk circled as if deciding if I were prey.

I had been looking for edible weeds. Only chickweed and bittercress were ready to harvest.

"Vitus Swinggate!" The voice penetrated the whistling wind in the grass. "We know yer there on account of your horse! Show yer self."

Thoreau was a few yards from me chomping on grass.

I stood to see that it was McKlusky with a big fella named Chuck at his side. Chester, Addie, and a few other kids from the McEwen house stood several paces behind them. Chester shrugged his shoulders and shook his head. Addie's eyes were red from crying.

"You're trespassin'," I said to McKlusky. "Whatcha want?"

"Chucky here, is fixin' to teach you a lesson." McKlusky's beady eyes narrowed over his nasty grin. Chucky was a good six inches taller than me and carried a considerable girth. He was easily three years my senior.

"I don't need any learnin', but thanks."

"You'll get it anyhow. And we're going to take that horse with us too."

"McKlusky," I said through gritted teeth, my temper growing, "You're nothing but a yellow belly son of a sow!"

I wasn't about to stand down now. My honor and my horse were on the line. And Addie was in the audience. I took a couple steps toward Chucky, straightening my back and puffing out my chest trying to look bigger.

We circled for a few seconds sizing each other up. Suddenly, he threw his closest fist at my face followed by the other. I easily parried both and followed up with a right punch of my own. I grazed his temple.

We exchanged a flurry of punches and kicks. I landed a

few good shots. He landed only one. I felt in control. My confidence soared. I lunged forward to punch him as he caught me in the floating ribs with a very strong kick. I doubled over in pain for an instant. Just long enough for him to charge me. He picked me up in a bear hug and tried to squeeze the remaining breath from me. As he lifted, I crushed his nose with a head butt loosening his grip.

My feet back on the ground, I wrapped my hands around the back of his neck and pulled him to me and delivered several knee strikes to his mid-section. He pushed away and I let him take a few steps back where he could regain his composure for a moment.

He inched toward me like a snake poised to strike. I kicked him in the side of the leg just above the knee with my shin. His leg buckled, but he recovered. His face was full of blood and fury. He came at me with a barrage of punches. I ducked under them and exploding forward with my legs, drove my shoulder into his stomach. I simultaneously grabbed the back of his knees and lifted him onto my shoulder as I had done before with animals after a successful hunt. I caught a glimpse of our audience with their jaws hanging open. They were surprised by my strength. I made a slight turn and slammed him onto the ground, driving my shoulder into his ribs. A terrible gasp escaped his mouth on impact.

I slid up and sat on his chest and started punching him in the face. He tried to block and punch back. He bucked his hips and thrashed wildly to get me off. He drove his knee into my spine throwing my weight forward. He grabbed my hair and yanked it toward the ground rolling me off. I hung onto him with my thighs, forcing him to roll with me.

I was now on my back with him between my legs. He tried to stand, but I crossed my ankles behind his back and pulled him back down to me. Like a caged animal, he began to go crazy. He started raining punches down, hitting my stomach and face. He lifted me off the ground and slammed me into the dirt, knocking the breath from my lungs.

I grabbed his neck and pulled myself closer to him where I could wrap my arm around his neck and under his chin. I cinched a chokehold tight enough to kill him. He squirmed and fought.

He lifted me and slammed me down again, but I only tightened my hold. His body softened. "Do you give up?" I yelled.

He responded with a weak punch to my ribs with his loose hand. I yanked on his neck again. "Say uncle!" My arm burned, but I held tight until he was totally limp. I released him from my hold and rolled him off. He looked dead.

I kneeled beside him to survey the damage. His face looked like he'd been trampled by horses. I was afraid I'd killed him. He looked like the Johnny Reb that died in front of Chester and me by the Harpeth.

Everyone else ran over. Finally, his chest heaved. And I let out a sigh of relief. He started coming to. When he propped himself on his elbows, I offered him my hand to help him up. He accepted. His head bowed and body slumped, he conceded I'd beaten him fair and square. He gave me a firm handshake and lumbered toward town, a deflated McKlusky in tow.

Addie and Chester sidled up beside me while the other kids left too.

"Here," Chester said as if the Chucky affair had never happened. "I thought I'd bring this along. The Colonel said you could probably use a good book by now."

It was a beat-up novel called *The Most Ancient and Famous History of the Renowned Prince Arthur*, by Sir Thomas Malory. I'd never heard of it, but I was glad to have a new paper friend.

I hobbled toward the barn holding Thoreau's reins in one hand and the book in the other. I was a little stunned when I felt Addie's arm wrap around mine. She looked at me with big green eyes that said she was there to help. I didn't mind.

THAT NIGHT, MA INVITED CHESTER AND ADDIE TO STAY FOR dinner. We had venison, of course, and had a few laughs along with it. Addie and I stole a few glances at each other between bites and pauses in conversation.

Afterward, out in the yard, Addie gave me a peck on the cheek before the two of them headed in to town.

"Walk her all the way to her house, will ya?" I called after Chester.

"Sure thing."

I took straight to the barn loft with a lantern and my new book. With Thoreau resting comfortably below me, I entered Sir Lancelot's world of sword fighting, jousting, and chivalry.

I read half the night in the loft before the intrigues of the Knights of the Round Table played out in my dreams. In the morning, I rooted around in the litter of used and broken farm implements around the barn until I found what I was looking for. It was an old axe handle, bound to the earth with fingers of grass. I yanked it free from the vegetation and spun it around in my hand. This will do, I thought.

I whittled the axe handle with my hunting knife until I had what resembled a dull sword blade and a workable grip. I bounced around to the back of the barn where I slashed and cut at low-hanging tree branches, twirling myself around as if fighting dozens of knights. Ma mixed eggshells and chicken poop into her small kitchen garden. If she noticed me at all, she didn't show it.

Having subdued the knights at the barn-castle, I mounted Thoreau and road him into the battlefield, swinging my sword at passing warriors, denting their armor, dismounting them. I jousted with champions, defeating them easily. All my actions were being observed by King Arthur himself and his bride Guinevere. More importantly, Princess Adelicia was there too, watching my heroics. I looked to the balcony on the castle for her nod of approval.

Thoreau and I galloped and slashed toward Camelot until we reached the home of the apprentice knight, Chester Hamm. He gawked at my sword with jealousy and listened with pure delight as I told of the adventures of Sir Lancelot.

"I guess I can tell the Colonel you're much obliged for the book?" Chester said.

"Why, yes, good sir. That would be most appreciated," I said with a bow.

I slashed at the tall grass with Excalibur. "How's everything at the McEwen House?"

"Ah, you know, same as usual." He sat on the crippled back steps of his house.

"McKlusky was bellyachin' about your run-in with Chucky. Said he was going to gather some fellas up to challenge you."

"I haven't time for such botherments," I said as I parried an imaginary sword attack.

"I'm serious, Vitus. He's fit to be tied and aims to do you some real harm."

"I'm pretty sure I made it quite clear yesterday I wasn't one to tangle with. He messes with me again, he'll be dead as a wagon wheel."

"But he's gathering a gang," he said with a hiccup. "You should make amends 'fore this whole thing gets out of hand. Come on, I'm headed to the McEwen House now. Come with me. The Colonel can help sort it out."

"First of all, I don't want the Colonel to know nothing about this. Second of all, I ain't worried about that pigeon liver McKlusky or his so-called gang. And thirdly, I'm not supposed to be out this way." Red rage gathered in my forehead. "I've gotta go. I'll see you around, Chester."

"See ya round."

Two mornings later, I found a sheet of paper nailed to the tree near the barn. It was a formal challenge issued by

McKlusky. We were to meet at noon the next day at Wilkin's barn.

A quiet laughed escaped me before I ripped it up and let it float into the grass. If seeing it increased my heart rate, it was imperceptible. I looked forward to yanking a knot in that little puppy's head.

I decided to leave Thoreau and Excalibur in the barn and took my time walking along the path toward Wilkin's barn the next day. I was a bit late for the appointed match, but I felt no rush. The forest was quiet save for the haunting song of a wood thrush echoing through the canopy. His melody signaled the end of winter and the beginning of planting season.

Everything had started turning green and budding leaves had already filled the gaps between branches, crowding the terrain enough that I didn't notice the five brutes crouching behind understory brush until they emerged.

Two had sticks, one had a knife, and the other two pounded their fists against their palms. I knew I was in trouble and immediately went to work. I gave the kid with the knife a solid kick in the chest, sending him into a grouping of ferns.

I turned to face the boys with the sticks. One swung and I blocked it with my left forearm, exciting a sharp pain in the outer bone. I tackled him. We both fell heavily into the rotting foliage. I began pounding on him, forgetting there were other assailants. Just as I turned to look for the other kids, a thick stick slammed into my head just above the temple with the loudest thud. I stood and then stumbled, the world a blur.

I felt another blow to the ribs. I blindly swung my fists, catching one kid in the jaw. More blows to my face, my stomach. A knife stab?

In my fading vision, McKlusky stood on the path with a smug look on his face. Everything went dark.

THIRTEEN

he got stabbed

I awoke in my bed. The house was quiet and empty. I sat up with an unimaginable amount of pain in my stomach. Bandages wrapped around my torso had a brown stain of blood just left of my belly button. *That sombitch did stab me.*

Pa was tilling the side field and Ma was tilling her small garden against the house.

"What are you doin' outta bed, young man?" she said when she noticed me on the porch steps. She pulled off her gloves as she approached.

"I...dunno. What happened? How'd I get here?"

"Well, apparently you got yourself into a tussle and didn't come out on the winning side." She smiled as she said it. "Doc says you'll make a full recovery. Says you were lucky the blade didn't hit any vital organs."

I must have looked confused.

"You don't remember?" she said as she stroked my cheek.

"Yeah, I remember getting ambushed by a bunch of cowards, but I don't remember anything after that."

"Well, by the grace of God, your friends Chester and Addie found you and brought you to the Wilkins house. Luckily, old man Wilkins practices healin'. He fixed you up the best he could and brought you back here. That was two days ago."

I didn't say anything, just watched Pa work the plow as Thoreau reluctantly pulled it along. I was glad to see Pa and my horse were getting along.

"You best be gettin' back to bed and get to healin'. We're gonna need your help as soon as you're fit. We're behind. The Wood thrush been singin' a week or more now. We gotta get sowin'."

I SPENT THE NEXT COUPLE WEEKS CONVALESCING. I HELPED with the chores as much as I could in the morning, gingerly sowing seeds in the afternoon, and reading at night. Occasionally, Chester and Addie came to see me. Chester caught me up on lessons I'd missed at the Colonel's and reported the goings-on of that turd McKlusky. Addie told me about her shenanigans with her girlfriends at the Franklin Female Institute. She'd sometimes hold my hand and tell me how sorry she was that McKlusky was so awful.

"It's between him and me," I said. "Don't bother your dad with it, okay?"

"He's already workin' up a good punishment for McKlusky. He might even put him behind bars for a few days."

"No," I said emphatically. "Tell him it's not McKlusky's fault."

"What? Are you mad?" Her big green eyes about drove me crazy, but it was a different kind of crazy.

"Just tell your dad to hold off…"

"But…"

"Tell him that piece of excrement deserves a trial or something. Something to stall him. I need to heal a little more."

"Heal. For what?" Her forehead crinkled.

"Never mind. Just don't worry about it."

"Well, we gotta go anyway. You rest and get better. Don't worry about McKlusky. And don't let your pa overwork you."

She gave me another kiss on the cheek and took off yelling for Chester to come along.

"Chester!" I said. "Hold on a sec." He sat beside me in the grass.

"Anything to report back in town?" I whispered.

"Nah, not really."

"Are you doing any spy work?"

"No, the Colonel told me to hold off for a bit. The bluebellies ain't been up to much lately. I guess the Colonel would rather until you're fixed up before we do spyin'."

"What about the man with the birthmark?" I asked.

"What about him?"

"Has he been around the McEwen house?"

"No, not that I've seen. Maybe he died in the fightin'."

"For my sake and Thoreau's, I hope he did." I felt a small twinge of guilt for thinking it, but it passed soon enough.

"Well, will ya please keep an eye out for him for me?" I asked.

"Got it, pard."

He ran off to catch up with Addie.

In the small hours of that night, I rode Thoreau up the road toward Chester's and dismounted a hundred yards from the house and crept to his bedroom window. The house was dark and quiet. I lightly tapped on the window until his face materialized behind the wavy glass. *Come out here*, I mouthed.

With a bang, he threw open the front door and met me beside their broken wagon that had been retired for five years or more.

Without preamble, I filled him in on my intentions. "I need you to tell McKlusky and his entire gang to meet me at the big sycamore tree in the graveyard two days from now just before sundown. He can even bring as many cowards as he wants. You got that?"

"Yes," he said as he wiped the sleep from his eyes. "Why would you want to do that? It didn't go so well for ya last time."

"Last time I was ambushed. This time I'll be ready."

"Are you sure yer up for it? With the knife wound and all?"

"I'm good enough."

"Why don't you wait a spell before committin' to something like that? You could very well die, Vit."

"The Colonel might lock him up. If he does, I won't get to exact my revenge."

"I don't know." His words stuttered. "Sounds like a bad idea."

"It'll work out. Will you tell him?"

He swiped at the grass with his bare foot. "Yeah, I guess I can. I want to be there with you, though."

I looked into his eyes. "That's fine, but only as a spectator, you hear. I don't want you tangled up in this. Promise?"

"Promise," he said weakly, head bowed.

"Will you tell him first thing and then come to my barn as soon as you can? I need to get some practice in."

"Practice? What pray tell are you yammerin' about now?"

"You'll see." I gave his shoulder a pat and took off into the dark.

FOURTEEN

I showed up at the sycamore tree over an hour before sunset, well before the scheduled battle. The tree was impressive. Its trunk possessed a girth that three grown men together could not connect fingers around. Its huge canopy sprawled overhead. The bottom branches almost stretched to the ground where giant, knobby roots reached toward the drip line. There were plenty of good limbs for a twelve-year-old boy to get a hold of.

I tucked Excalibur into the back of my belt and made my way up its scaly trunk into the web of limbs, pieces of bark tinkling to the ground below. The leaves, still only buds, didn't provide much cover. Some years before, lightning hit the top of the tree and set it on fire briefly. As the wood later rotted away, it left a large cavity. A cavity into which I fit snuggly.

I sat inside the hole, holding Excalibur, and waited.

As the sky in the west filled with swaths of purple and orange, voices rose from below me. First, McKlusky and his goons talking in a relaxed tone. One of them yelled, "Is your boy gonna show up?"

"You can bet your ass he will." It was Chester. His voice sounded thirty yards off. "And all of y'all are gonna regret it."

"You brought his girlfriend to watch him get beat to a pulp?" McKlusky said.

Addie had come too?

I sat listening to disparaging comments made about yours truly, until the light faded. I slowly extricated myself from inside the tree onto a thick limb, crouched, ready to spring.

"I guess the lily liver isn't coming," McKlusky said.

"He's coming, fart sniffer," Chester defended.

"It's dark. How we suppose to give him a proper beating now?"

Exactly, I thought.

Excalibur in my hand, I sprung from the tree, breaking my fall with someone's shoulder, collapsing him and rendering him useless. Before the rest of them even knew what was happening, I shot to the nearest person and broke his arm with a stroke of Excalibur. His silhouette collapsed with a piercing shriek of pain and fear.

Like startled deer, the others reeled away from the trunk of the sycamore pivoting their heads side to side in confusion. Excalibur felt natural in my hand, as if it had always been a part of me. I glided swiftly toward the crowd of enemies, Excalibur slashing in smooth strokes. I swung the wooden sword left to right and back with seamless fluidity. A swipe from the right across someone's thigh, a cut from the left on another's jaw.

Screams filled the night. Footfalls retreated into the growing dark. An outline matching the portly figure of McKlusky stood frozen between me and an open tomb. I ran at him, jumping the tomb, swinging Excalibur downward. McKlusky threw his hand up in panicked reaction. Excalibur broke his wrist and sunk into his forehead. A sickening thud as wood met bone. He collapsed in a silent pile. I looked down on him, panting.

I listened as multiple footsteps faded into the surrounding terrain in different directions. It was over already? The whole thing was a blur, as if I hadn't been a part of it. Like I had no control.

Looking down at the dark mass at my feet, fear suddenly gripped me. The hands of reality clutched my throat and quickened my heart. I may have killed him. I glanced toward Chester and Addie. In the dim lighting, I could make out Chester's open mouth and Addie's hands over her face.

I felt like an animal that had been cornered, forced to fight with wild abandon. Causing casualties with no regard for consequences. I was a savage beast. Like a wolf scared from its prey by a gunshot, I took off into the night.

THE FOLLOWING AFTERNOON, THE HINGES OF THE BARN DOOR creaked and daylight flooded into the understory. Chester's voice in the doorway.

"You up there?"

"Yeah," I muttered, feeling the shame of a criminal. I poked my head over the edge of the loft.

"Just came by to give you a casualty report." He flashed a sardonic smile. I fell back into the hay.

"No one's dead. Busted up purty bad though."

I let out a deep breath, my stab wound shooting pain throughout my torso. He climbed the ladder, pausing on the top rungs.

"Addie is out of kilter with the whole affair. Says you scared her real bad." I pretended to read my book. I didn't want to make eye contact.

"Vitus, you're in a might of trouble, you know."

"I assumed as much."

"The families of all those boys want resinution of some sort."

"Restitution," I corrected. "It's pronounced rest-i-tution."

"Whatever, Vit. The only reason they ain't here is cause of the Colonel. He's telling the families he'll take care of everything and they shouldn't meddle with official affairs. He's sayin' you're too dangerous for regular folk to pursue and that they just need to let him handle it.

"Course, I don't know how long that will last. They could lose patience and come after you anyway."

"To hell with all of 'em!" I felt the blood in my head heat up. "They came askin' for trouble, and I gave it to 'em. They ain't innocent either." I pointed at my stab wound.

"Their injuries are worse than your normal tussle. It ain't just black eyes and hurt feelin's. There's broken bones and big ole' gashes involved here. Hell, McKlusky ain't right in the head yet."

"He never had much going on upstairs anyway," I grumbled as I turned a page.

"I haven't got to the worst part yet." What's worse than Addie hating me, I thought.

"Yeah, what's that."

"The Colonel don't want you to come around no more on account of most those boys livin' there. No more missions either. Said you can't serve too well as a spy if half the town's lookin' for ya."

This was a punch in the gut. So much of me revolved around the McEwen house. It was my second home, my education, my social center, my headquarters.

"Ya just took it too far, pal."

Chester knew I was on the verge of tears. To spare me the embarrassment, he quietly climbed down the ladder. He patted Thoreau and walk out. Just beyond the door, he called up, "I'll come check on you in a day or two."

He closed the barn door, shutting out the light. I did indeed cry.

FIFTEEN

I lay in the loft until dusk waiting for the lynch mob. No one came, not even Ma and Pa. I had grown very antsy lying around feeling sorry for myself and fearing the worst. Eventually, I decided I needed to find out one way or another what my future held.

I strapped Excalibur to my back with a leather strap and left the barn. A muted glow on the curtains suggested Ma was in the kitchen.

I took my time walking on the road toward Franklin, not sure exactly what I was going to do. I ambled in the dark, my bare feet finding wagon tracks. There was no moon. Katydids hummed and stars twinkled. Ahead to my left, the gargled song of frogs indicated I was nearing the swamp. As I came alongside, they went silent. I listened to the stillness.

A dog barked from a nearby farm, followed by another in town. This set off a chorus of coyotes encircling me. Their eerie howls, resembling laughing witches, echoed throughout the surrounding hills. I squatted on my haunches to rethink my expedition. I suddenly felt very alone. Vulnerable to attacks from wild animals or bandits.

I remained squatting in the road for twenty deep breaths, listening. The frogs began singing again. First just one or two, then hundreds. They surrounded me, a din of peeps and trills. I thought I'd try to continue on slowly and quietly, using the frogs as my measure of stealth. I made it beyond the swamp without disturbing the frogs again.

I continued slowly along the road until the dark outline of hills behind Chester's house revealed themselves. I carried on in a trance until a blur of faint light materialized and slowly became apparent. It was a camp fire. Its light danced on four canvas tents. Several other tents stood outside the reach of the light. Yankees sat around the fire jabbering and drinking.

I was lucky to have noticed them before they spotted me. I disappeared into a field and circumnavigated their position.

A faint light from a window of the McEwen house cut through the murk ahead of me. I crept through the yard to the side of the meat house. Inside, Mammy was scraping pots. It smelled as if she had been boiling onions.

Keeping my eye on the glow in one of the downstairs windows, I crouch-ran to the back porch. I slowly overtook the stairs and tested the planks. Staying on the edges where the boards were less prone to squeak, I moved like a ghost to the lighted window.

A candelabra cast a deep yellow on the family portrait and antique clock. No one was in the room, but there were faint voices deep within. I crept around to another window closer to the front of the house and looked in just as the Colonel walked out of the room. I pulled myself higher on the sill and craned my neck to see if there was anyone else in the room. No one.

Before I could drop down, the Colonel came back in and must have seen my shape out of the corner of his eye. He ran to the window, but only after I had disappeared into the shadows. The side porch door flew open. "Who's out there?" He had a fire iron in one hand and a lantern in the other. "Show yourself, you Yankee bastard!"

I lay just below him against the porch in the very shadow his lantern cast, holding my breath. A man's voice came from the dark front yard.

"What is it, sir? What's all the racket?"

I could tell from his silhouette that the man was wearing a Union uniform.

"If you bluebellies are going to guard my house, you best keep away from the windows! I'm not putting up with peeping toms!"

"Well, sir I assure you—"

The Colonel slammed the door.

I lay still and watched until the guard returned to the front porch.

I let out a breath of relief. I surged with adrenaline. After checking to make sure neither one was still looking, I ran across the yard, hopping the boxwoods. I turned back in time to see the Colonel drawing the curtains on all the downstairs windows.

My body continued to buzz from the excitement. I wanted more. I headed down Bridge Street, keeping to shadows, toward the McKlusky house. No lights showed through the windows. I froze when I noticed a man rocking in a chair on a porch across the street. He was smoking a cigarette. It didn't smell like the tobacco substitutes Franklin citizens were forced to use. It smelled sweeter.

That's when I realized it was a Union soldier sitting on the porch, not more than twenty yards from me. There seemed to be Yankee guards everywhere. Without notice, his head turned toward me.

"Hey, you there." He stood and threw the glowing butt into the grass. "What are you doing out!"

I turned on my heel and ran for my life.

"Hey, get back here! Stop!" His boots hammered the wood steps and then the cobbles. I took the corner around a house and shot up Main Street. His footfalls picked up pace behind me. As I crossed Bridge Street, I was spotted by a sentry a few doors down.

"Halt!" one of them yelled.

I accelerated. My unprotected feet burned from the pounding, finding relief in the grass of the city cemetery. On the opposite side, between me and the river, was another Yankee encampment. More voices called out from behind me.

I found Colonel Guilford Dudley's tomb with the slightly opened lid. Being caught out past curfew carried a pretty stiff penalty, but my activities could be interpreted as espionage, which could result in hanging. My decision was easy. I pulled the stone lid, grinding loudly, until the gap was wide enough to accommodate me. I lowered myself into the tomb and slid it shut, leaving a small space for ventilation.

The darkness was complete. I couldn't see my hand in front of my face. The smell of mud and rot was overpowering. I stuck my nose into the crack to breath in some outside air. I waited several minutes listening to voices throughout the cemetery. When they died down, I surmised they'd given up the hunt. I pulled the lid back a few more inches, fresh air pouring in.

The ground beneath me was soft, the atmosphere dank and overwhelmingly creepy. I did not feel alone. I prayed that a past flooding of the Harpeth had flushed out the remains and carried them miles away, and whatever poked at my back was a root and not one of Dudley's bones. I was afraid to move. I pictured a soldier sitting on a headstone smoking another cigarette, watching me.

Despite the disturbing situation in which I'd found myself, I dozed off. When I awoke, I had no way to tell how long I'd slept, but I knew it was long enough. I grasped the lid, pressing my knees against the wall, and pulled it open. The sound of stone on stone was deafening.

I emerged from the tomb like Polidori's *Vampyre*, pivoting my head to check for the soldiers. I was alone with the headstones. I took a few deep breaths and moved among the graves like a phantom. I made short work of getting back to the road and managing my way home.

The thrill of sneaking around town at night lured me from home again the next night. If the Colonel didn't want me spying during the day for fear I'd be seen, I figured I'd see what I could find out at night.

I moved more quietly and swiftly. The frogs in the

swamp paid no notice of my muted steps. They sang as if I wasn't even there. No dogs were aroused, giving me more confidence in my abilities as a covert agent. My first mission was to learn how many Union soldiers were in town, occupying our buildings.

I stalked outside of the fire light of their encampments and lanterns of guards. From the shadows, I'd listen to conversations held by men in their camps or the huddled groups on patrol.

The McEwen house was dark so I slipped past it toward town square where I shimmied to the top of a building. I peered over the roof. Men in blue walked around the streets as if they owned them. Laughing and play fighting. Going in and out of the stores and bars swaying with drunkenness. I just lay there and watched, my stomach turning.

When I'd had my fill, I slipped off the roof into the alley and darted into the moonlit fields. To avoid the road and Yankee camps, I walked silently through the soft, recently turned soil until I made it back to my barn and Thoreau.

For the next month or so, I prowled around town at night as often as I could after spending most of the day plowing and sowing with Pa. I kept a tally on Union soldiers, noting the number of new faces.

I became increasingly brave each night I went out. When the light from the moon was minimal, I'd test my stealth skills. I'd get as close to Yankee camps as I could, find a tree stump, lump of soil, patch of grass, or even sometimes a wagon wheel. When I felt sufficiently hidden, I'd throw a rock or stick at their tents until they took notice enough to stand and walk around to investigate.

As they stumbled around blindly, I'd remain as still as the object I hid behind, part of its shadow. At times, they'd walk within feet of me unaware of my presence. I took great delight knowing if I had a knife or garrote, I could have easily killed a few Invaders.

One night, the moon was merely a sliver, the streets of Franklin ink black. I followed a lone sentry down Cameron Street toward the cemetery. I lured him farther from homes and buildings by throwing small pieces of iron I'd found behind the blacksmith shop.

I'd throw one into the street ahead of him. He held his lantern out in front of his face as he followed the sound. I'd throw another, farther down the street.

"Who's there?" he called out. He turned in my direction. Feeling bold, instead of diving behind something, I stood very still on the side of the road like a statue. He didn't notice me. He returned his attention toward the sounds. His movements displayed a discomfort. His gait seemed agitated and anxious. When he couldn't find the source of the noise, he started back in my direction, his pace quickened with fear.

I threw another piece of iron behind him, hitting the side of a brick house. He again stopped in his tracks and turned away from me in search of this insistent noise.

"Show yourself!"

I followed him a few paces behind, watching the lantern light sway to and fro. A black replica of his form stretched out behind him, growing and shrinking as the lantern swung. I stayed just beyond his shadow, close enough to hear his panting.

In that moment, I was empowered knowing how easily I could snuff the life from him before he even knew the reaper stood behind him. I had no weapon, nor did I have enough motivation to murder a man in cold blood in the streets of my town. But I could have. That notion alone sparked something in my blood.

This sentry was, by all accounts, an enemy. To me, walking behind him in the dark, he was no more than frightened prey, and I a predator stalking him. His vulnerability made me feel a bit of compassion for him.

What was my real grievance toward this man and the rest of the Invaders? Sure, they stole our pigs and our horses without payment or receipt. They have invaded our homes, eaten our food, and littered the streets. But isn't that just the way of war? Are the Confederate armies innocent of the same exploits? Unlikely. Guerrilla Rebel parties and bandits have done their fair share of misdeeds on their own soil. Even here in Franklin.

So, I had no pressing desire to dispatch this man. The thrill of knowing I could do what I pleased had I the inclination and then vanish like a ghost was enough to keep me coming back night after night to pester the Yankees.

When I wasn't harassing Invaders, I eavesdropped on dozens of conversations, mostly benign, but a handful proved noteworthy. Once a week, I'd meet Chester at the bend of the Harpeth where the white, tangled roots of a sycamore spread over the water like an umbrella. We'd sit on top dangling our fishing lines in its shadow. I'd relay the information to Chester and ask him to tell the Colonel in hopes I'd win back his approval.

Chester, working as a liaison, maintained a very spotty line of communication between the Colonel and me. He said the Colonel appreciated my covert operations, but had no real use for them.

"He still cares about you, Vit," Chester would say, "but he's of the mind he can't fraternate with you on account of most of the parents in town wantin' your head on a spit. He's still covern' for you best he can."

"Fraternize," I corrected.

"Huh?"

"Nothing."

"I hate sayin' it, Vit, but he's got a point. Parents show up at the McEwen house nearly every day askin' for ya. Heck a few even asked me to tell them where you lived. I told em' to get lost."

"Thanks, buddy," I said as I patted his shoulder, hot from the blistering sun. "What about the fart sniffer?"

"He still ain't sniffin' anything really. He just barely woke. The doctor says his brain don't work right anymore."

"Never did." I felt a pang of guilt.

"I know he was a turd, Vit, but that's purty serious."

"I know." I watched my dangling feet swing over the water, wondering why I didn't feel more remorse.

SIXTEEN

"Vit! Vit!" Chester crashed through the barn door.

"What is it?" I yelled from behind my latest book, Daniel Defoe's *Robinson Crusoe*. Chester had taken it from the Colonel's library and brought it to me a few days before.

"Hi, Thoreau." Panting, he flew up the ladder. "They caught two spies! The Yankees caught em some spies!"

I slammed my book shut and stared at him. My feelings were mixed. This was bad for the Confederates, but exciting for two young boys.

"What are we gonna do 'bout it?" he asked.

"Chester, what do you mean what are we going to do about it? What's to be done?"

"What if they know 'bout our missions?"

That's when it dawned on me that Chester and I were spies too, just as guilty. We could be compromised. Fear wrapped its cold hands around my throat. I gave it a moment's thought.

"Nah, we're just harmless kids. They can't do nothing to us even if they knew we were up to something." I feared there was more comfort in that statement than truth.

"Find out what you can and meet me here tomorrow morning. You mind doin' that?"

"No," he said, and bolted back to town.

LIKE A FAITHFUL DOG, CHESTER SHOWED UP THE NEXT morning. He walked the fields with me as I plucked weeds and re-covered sprouts deer or skunks had dug up the night before.

"Well," Chester started, " 'parently the spies were adults who dressed up as Union big shots. Said they was there to inspect Fort Granger. It almost worked too, but Colonel Baird wasn't havin' it."

"What'd they do to 'em'?"

"Trial first thing in the mornin'. The Colonel said they'll hang for sure."

"Do you know where?"

"No."

"Probably at the fort," I said.

"Yeah."

"Can you do me another favor, pard?"

"Sure, Vit, what is it?"

"This is a big one."

"Shoot." He rubbed a hand over his mouth.

"I gotta see this happen. I gotta know what's goin' on."

"Yeah, me too."

"Since I can't be seen in town, I'll have to watch from afar."

"How you spose to do that?"

"Can you stay at the McEwen's tonight?" I asked, wondering if I was asking for too much from my friend.

"Yeah, but what's that got to do with anything?"

"I want you to borrow the Colonel's field glasses for me."

"Oh, now wait a minute pard—"

I held a finger up. "Just listen. You can give them right back."

He rolled his eyes.

"I'll meet you behind the meat house at midnight. I can climb into the bell tower, sleep there, then watch the whole thing from there with the field glasses."

"Don't cha want me to come?"

"Sure, you can come with me, I'd 'preciate the company, but remember, you can go and see it in person."

He smiled, remembering he had the freedom I didn't enjoy.

"Whud ya say, pard?" I said.

"Okay. Midnight."

That night was clear under a half moon. Chester was a few minutes late to the meat house, but he had the prize in hand.

"The Colonel said the spies'll be hangin' at Fort Granger midmorning. I think I'll watch the trial with everyone else," he said.

"After thinkin' on it, you're right. If the Colonel notices the field glasses are gone, and so are you, well then you're done for. Wish me luck."

"Good luck," he whispered as I stood and ran full clip to St. Paul's.

I distracted the guards by throwing a stone at a trash heap across the street. It hit something hard, making a racket. When they left their posts to investigate, I used footholds in the church's ornate brick design to scale the wall to the roof, then the tower. Dozens of swallows flew from the opening, squeaking and fluttering, nearly knocking me from the wall. I slid inside the tower.

There was a small ledge, just wide enough to accommodate my back end. I leaned against the cool brick, enjoying the breeze flowing from one opening to the other. The large bell hung beside me motionless. The brick of the inner walls were lightly coated in soot and smelled like a chimney.

I awoke at first light, my leg dangling from the ledge into the dark abyss of the tower. Voices from the sanctuary below floated up the shaft like smoke from a stovepipe. Mostly everyday kind of talk. Nothing to get excited about. During pauses in conversation, the faint sound of hammering echoed off nearby buildings. I looked toward Figuer's Bluff with the field glasses. In a clearing near the fort, men hoisted scaffolding onto a cherry tree.

A few hours later, soldiers escorted two men out the gates of the fort. Hundreds of Yankees surrounded the place of execution, solemn looks on their faces. The two spies were blindfolded and made to stand in a cart where nooses were placed around their necks. One man was crying, the other seemed to be consoling him verbally and grabbed his hand just before a horse yanked the cart out from under them. The rope jerked their necks violently and grotesquely as they fell. A cascade of leaves floated down around them. Heads of onlookers turned from the gruesome display.

Their bodies twitched and gyrated, urine poured out the bottom of their trousers legs. They swung back and forth under the branches of the cherry tree for many minutes before they were cut down. The bodies were placed in plain coffins and carried off.

My stomach rolled and heaved at the cruelty. Their death was much less honorable than taking a bullet during a heated battle. The public execution of two men in front of hundreds of spectators made me sadder and angrier than the other deaths I'd seen in recent months.

I sat in the bell tower for a while unable to shake the image of the two men hanging from the cherry tree. Something had stirred in me that wasn't there before. A niggling of vengeance and hatred.

The door of the McEwen house slammed, pulling me from my reverie. It was Addie. She walked across the yard in a light blue dress and white bonnet, holding a couple of books to her chest. Mammy was in tow. They walked single file until Mammy saw to it that Addie had made it safely to the Franklin Female Institute. Mammy then walked past me into town.

That's when I realized I was stuck there in the tower until dark. I failed to think my extraction through with detail. I hadn't even brought food. It would be a long day. My legs were already cramped. I stifled a whine before it made its way through my lips.

I managed to doze off. I woke to the sound of voices in the McEwen yard across the street. The afternoon sun penetrated through a slot in the tower, heating my thigh. The McEwen sisters and a few boys were playing hide and seek. Addie ran from the side of the house and ducked behind a bush near the road. I wanted to yell, "Hi, Addie. Up here!" but knew what would happen if I did. I just watched her, crouched in her hiding spot, head down between her knees, a smile on her face.

I would have given a hefty sum to play too. All I could do was pretend I was involved. I had the ultimate hiding spot. A spot where no one would ever find me. Where no call of "all in come free" could ever draw me out.

Chester ran around the corner of the house chasing Roger, who had a bandaged arm, presumably from his encounter with Excalibur. Chester paused for a moment and looked up at the bell tower. I gave him a small wave. Afraid to give me away, he just gave a little nod.

I'd never felt so lonely.

Darkness slowly descended over the town. Horses trotted to a stop below me in the courtyard. Men's voices told me the Yankees were back for the night. I waited and listened for the church to become quiet, my legs growing numb.

It was hours before the last voice fell silent. I sat a little longer before I made my move. I decided down-climbing the brick would prove dangerous, so I grabbed the rope of the bell and pulled it very slowly until the clapper lay against the side of the bell. I added more and more weight until I could hang on it without the bell betraying me with its song. The rope slid between my hands, burning a little. I paused my descent, my feet dangling just above the ceiling. Still quiet.

I lowered myself through the opening in the plaster and onto the floor of the narthex. The usual smell of oiled wood, beeswax candles, and leather had been replaced by the smell of burnt wood, excrement, and body odor. A snort and cough echoed through the church. I slowly took my weight off the rope. *Don't ring. Please don't ring.*

Through a crack in the door, I watched a few candles flicker in the sanctuary. The pews were missing. Snores floated across the space. As I stepped into the nave, something on my right moved and thudded on the wood floor.

I waited a few breaths, then took another careful step forward. The planks below me creaked despite my efforts to tread lightly. To my left, a Yankee stirred on his bedroll. Several more lay motionless, scattered about.

The pulpit, woodwork, and all of the pews had disappeared. Where the lectern once stood, remnants of a large fire smoked lazily. They had used most of the wood to keep warm.

The pew my family had sat on was now a pile of ashes. The last time I had sat in that church, I spent much of the service looking at the large red bow in Addie's hair. The bow rotated as her eyes wandered during the sermon. The bright silk bobbed up and down when she sang hymns. Occasionally, she'd turn in the pew and look past me at nothing in particular, then flash me a quick smile as her eyes met mine. She'd then yank her head back toward the pulpit.

Chester, sitting in the same row as the McEwens, swiveled and stuck his tongue out at me. My brother, James kicked the side of my shin, reminding me to pay attention. The pews had been uncomfortable, but everyone

I had cared about once occupied them. Those pews and that memory had gone up in smoke. All that was left was a black ghost on the ceiling. It spread dark arms toward the front of the church, growing faint as it made its way up the tower.

The organ pipes were torn apart, many missing. Large gouges marred the main columns where they'd affixed water troughs for the horses. Piles of dry horse crap littered the nave. A hot pressure built up in my skull. If I killed these sleeping Yankees—

A man turned in his sleep and coughed. My chest caved with a breath. If the Yankees woke up to find me there, they'd kill me. I couldn't take them all on.

I hurried to the front of the church and cracked the door open. A patrol of four men were walking past. I waited until they were out of sight, and ran off into the night.

I didn't slow until I'd made it back to my barn. I struggled up the ladder and collapsed in my hay pile without telling Thoreau goodnight.

SEVENTEEN

A man's voice from the dooryard woke me around midmorning. I peeked through cracks in the barn wall to see Ma and Pa standing near the back door greeting the Colonel who held his hat in his hands. The Colonel never visited us out here. My heart was in my throat. Was this about the McKlusky affair? My nighttime adventures? They invited him inside.

I didn't know whether I should flee or face the music. After some consideration, I stood. The leather strap of the Colonel's field glasses rubbed my neck as they thumped heavily on my chest. That was it. He was here for the glasses. I could just explain what happened. He wouldn't be too sore. Just in case, I tucked them under the hay with my rifle and Excalibur. I descended the ladder, crossed the yard, and opened the kitchen door. The three of them were sitting at the table.

"Hi there, son," the Colonel said. Love and dread showed in his eyes. "I guess you need to hear this too." My palms were slippery with sweat. *God, please don't let this be what I think.*

"Well, go ahead Mr. McEwen," Ma said with a shaky voice. "We're all ears." She was shaking with anxiety. Pa grabbed her hand.

"You all know Tod Carter has been corresponding—"

"Yeah, what about it, Mr. McEwen," Ma interrupted. "Get on with it."

The Colonel shifted in his seat.

"Fountain Branch showed me a letter Tod had sent a little while back asking that I deliver the message to you. Well, as you might expect, Tod and James were together a great deal, along with George Hamm and Bubba McKlusk—"

"Damn it, Mr. McEwen!" Pa yelled as he slammed his fist on the table. "No offense, but tell us straight away why you're here!"

"Mr. and Mrs. Swinggate, James is dead."

Ma collapsed on the floor in a pile, shrieking, "God, no! Please, God, no!" Pa was stunned into silence. The Colonel kept talking, pushing through, his words watery and muffled.

"He was killed in a skirmish somewhere between Murfreesboro and Chattanooga during a cavalry raid."

Pressure built behind my eyes. I wasn't thinking. I crashed through the back door into the dooryard and kept running through the fields crying and screaming. I had no control over myself. I only slowed enough to kick saplings and punch cattails. I kept running until I started up a wooded hill and grew exhausted.

I pressed uphill until I found a large stack of square,

moss-covered rock at the top. Pa, James, and I had rested here on a hunting trip a few years back. I remember hopping from rock to rock and Pa saying, "This pile of rock is an Indian grave yard, son. Show it respect."

Embarrassed, I sat next to James. He squeezed my shoulder. "Here try this." He turned to Pa, "Can he try the coffee?"

Pa nodded. I took a sip and spewed it all over a cube-shaped rock the size of my torso.

"Damn it, son!" Pa barked. "I just told you to respect this place."

James laughed.

"You better ask for forgiveness," Pa demanded.

James kept laughing and laughing. Soon Pa and I shared a giggle.

The laughter was only an echo of the past. There was nothing to laugh about now. I crumpled on the rocks and wept. *Why did you let this happen, God?*

I SPENT HOURS IN THE FOREST THAT DAY, CRYING AND HITTING trees with sticks until I gave in to exhaustion. I fell asleep on a soft patch of moss warmed by the sun through a small gap in the lush canopy.

At dusk, a bluejay called harshly, starting me awake. I lumbered back toward home, heavy with sorrow. I couldn't bear to see my folks so distraught, so I entered the dark barn. I patted Thoreau's neck and hugged his muzzle, before climbing into the loft.

Reaching into the hay, I felt the cold steel of the Whitworth, then found Excalibur and hugged it to me like a baby doll.

THE NEXT MORNING, I COULD NO LONGER AVOID MY PARENTS. It wasn't fair of me to run off like that. Inside the house was quiet. I found Ma lying in bed on her side facing the window.

"Ma, you okay?"

No response.

I went around the bed to see her face. She stared blankly.

"Ma. Where's Pa?"

No answer. She was a complete picture of despondency. I ran my hand up and down the quilt covering her arm before I left her alone.

Pa was nowhere to be found on the farm so I headed into town. I slowed when Chester came running from his house to greet me on the road.

"Hey, Vit." He kicked a stone across the dirt tracks. "Gosh, I sure am sorry, buddy. He was like a brother to me too." He offered me a hand shake. I ignored it and started walking again.

"You seen my pa?" I asked, eyes toward town.

"No, I ain't seen him. But where you goin'? You can't go to town. They're after you still."

"I need to find my pa."

As we approached the Yankee encampment, I squatted on the road to deliberate my approach. Chester dropped down behind me. A small line of smoke rose from the black coals of an untended fire. The camp was empty. We walked cautiously to get a closer look.

"No one's here," Chester said as he threw back a tent flap. "And look, what in hell's that about?" He pointed at a patch of dirt stained with blood. "What in tarnation's goin' on, you think?"

I didn't know, but something didn't feel right.

"I aim to find out," I said as I hustled up the road. Chester ran up from behind and grabbed my shoulder, spinning me around.

"Listen, it's too dangerous for you. You go back home and take care of your ma. Your pa may even be there somewheres too. Let me find out what's goin' on and I'll come back and tell ya."

Chester was right. It was foolish to go into town during the day.

"Yeah, I guess you're right." I said. "I do need to tend to Ma."

I trusted Chester more than anyone. He knew how to sneak around town unnoticed. He'd do anything for me.

"Come back and tell me what you find out the minute you learn something, okay?"

"Yeah, Vit I'll come back straight away."

I watched him run until he disappeared into the streets of Franklin.

Ma was still in bed when I got back. The shape of her lump under the quilt looked unmoved. I went outside and collected a handful of fleabane to make her some tea.

"Here, Ma. This will make you feel better."

She grumbled incoherently.

"Ma, where's Pa?"

Another grumble, almost sounding like words.

"Ma, I need to know were Pa is."

"He left," she finally said, more into her pillow.

"Where'd he go?"

"Kill Yankees."

My heart pounded. I left her room and removed the floorboards near the fireplace where Pa had hidden his rifle from Union trespassers. The cavity underneath was empty. My mind spun. I didn't know what to do. So I did the only thing I could think to do.

I ran to the barn, jumped on Thoreau, and we flew into the fields to the west. I tried to focus on the feeling of the wind on my face, the sound of his hooves drumming in the dirt, and the smell of dust and horse sweat. I rode until I felt a sufficient amount of time had passed for Chester to finish his reconnoitering and get back with his report.

The farm was quiet when I returned. Ma hadn't moved and Chester hadn't come back.

I practiced sword fighting with the lower leaves of a sugar maple until Chester appeared on the horizon. I ran to meet him.

"It's not good, Vit."

"Tell me, Chester."

"I talked to the Colonel. The bluebellies have your pa."

"What? Why?"

"'Parently, he shot and killed one."

I sat in the dirt, hands on my head.

"Said, he walked right up to the camp raving something about his boy and got off one shot before the Yankees put two bullets in him. One in the leg, one in the body somewheres. They dragged him off."

"But, he's alive?"

"For now, I spose."

"Do you know where they have him?" Tears welled. I blinked them away.

"They got him at the Mason Lodge." He sat beside me and put his arm across my shoulders.

"I know you've had a rough run, pard, but we'll get through this together."

"Thanks, pard." I wiped my nose on my sleeve.

"From what I can tell, the Colonel is gonna do his lawyer thing to help yer pa."

"I just don't see how that will help."

"Well, for now, let's just cross our fingers. How's yer ma?"

"Same."

That night, I tried to stay with Ma to comfort her. Even if she hadn't completely ignored me, I still wouldn't have been able to resist making a midnight visit to the Mason's Lodge. I stole away under a full moon, Excalibur strapped to my back.

As I neared town, it became obvious that the federal presence had increased since Pa's attack. Lights of several different patrols moved between houses and buildings. Hiram Mason Lodge was only a hundred yards from the bridge to Nashville, so I took to the banks of the Harpeth and followed it until I was in back of the lodge.

It was an imposing structure. It was one of the first three-story buildings in Tennessee. Gaining access to the roof before the Union occupation had been relatively easy. But over the last several months, the lodge had been used as a Yankee barracks. Groups of guards stood in the gold circles of lampposts.

I hadn't even decided what I was planning to do. I think I just wanted to see Pa. Maybe get a glance through a window. See if he was still alive.

The longer I lay in the grass watching dozens of guards going to and fro, the more my desire to infiltrate abated. Eventually, I gave up on the idea. It was a fool's errand to try and get anywhere near that building. Maybe Chester could find something out.

Defeated, I slid back down the bank and took my time walking home. I stayed inside the house that night to be with Ma, but I didn't think she even noticed.

The next morning, I found a couple eggs in the coop and cooked them up for Ma. She refused them, so I sat on the floor beside the bed and ate them myself.

"Is he dead?" Her voice was quiet and raspy. I didn't know if she was questioning the death of James or if she was referring to Pa.

"I said, is your pa dead?"

"I don't know, Ma. I just know he's been shot but is still alive."

"He's as good as dead."

"Ma, Mr. McEwen is going to help."

"Ain't nothing can be done."

"Ma, you really should eat something."

"Go away."

I left her and stood in the dooryard momentarily, breathing deeply. It smelled of approaching rain. I walked the fields, checking on the crops. The peas were close to maturity; I plucked a small pod and tossed it in my mouth. The beans were coming along according to schedule and the corn was as high as my hips.

A drop of rain smacked the soil. Then another and another until the sky opened up above me. The devil must have been beating his wife because the sun shone brightly to the west.

I walked to the barn where I lay in the loft reading *Robinson Crusoe*, listening to the rain patter on the roof. I couldn't give Mr. Crusoe his due attention. Thoughts of Pa and Ma distracted me from his adventures. What was going to happen to Pa? How was I going to tend to this farm on my own? Would Ma ever recover from the loss of James, or would she just wither away in that dirty old house?

The rain didn't last very long. I went back out and grabbed a handful of early peas, and brought them back for Ma. She refused them, so I ate them myself.

The next morning I realized it was Friday, so after my chores, I decided to go see if Chester was home. Often, on Fridays, Chester would stay with his pa.

He was sitting on the old wagon whittling a stick.

"I woulda come see ya, but I got nothin' to report." He peeled off a flake of bark from his stick.

"The Colonel doesn't even have nothin' to say?"

"No, he's of the mind that the Yankees are gonna let him rot for a spell."

"He's wounded! Are they even going to treat him?"

"Like I said, I don't know nothing else, Vit. Sorry. Spose that could be part of the punishment. Just let 'em suffer."

Neither of us spoke for a moment, he kept chipping away at the stick. I picked up an acorn.

"I have to do something." I flung it as far as I could.

"There's nothin' can be done. The lodge is heavily guarded."

"I know. I was there the other night."

"You might want to consider retirin' from your clementine missions, Vit."

"Clandestine."

"Whatever, you know what I mean. You had better be careful. Those parents still want to kill you, and you're the son of a … well, I hate sayin' it… convicted killer. Everyone's gonna keep an eye out for ya."

"I know, you're right. Just let me know when you hear something, will ya, pard?"

"Of course."

"You wanna go frog giggin' at the Campbell pond?" I asked, needing to do something to keep my mind at bay.

"Sure as shootin'!"

The house was stifling and smelled like mildew and rot. I opened the windows throughout, allowing a summer breeze to wash through the small house.

"You eaten anything lately, Ma?" I asked as I opened the window she stared blankly through from bed. She gave me no response. My patience waning, I bent over, eye to eye with her.

"I'm your son too, you know! James is gone, but I'm still here!"

She turned to her other side.

"Ma, I'm all you've got. You're all I've got. But you keep carrying on like this and I'll be all alone. Doesn't that matter to you? I'm here in the flesh, in your flesh and blood, yet you ignore me so you can waste away while focusing on those who are gone."

She pulled the quilt higher on her shoulder. I yelled and punched the wall, then went outside, slamming the door. I had tied Thoreau to the maple to give him shelter from the sun. He looked up at the sound of the door, then returned to rooting around in the dark green grass in the shade.

A whistle came from my left. Chester. I waved to him and he started running up the road to me.

"What's the matter?" he asked, no doubt noticing the chagrin on my face.

"Ma's gone."

"Dead?"

"Might as well be. She don't give a tinker's damn I'm still around."

"Flim flam. She cares 'bout you, she's just sick in the head." He looked up then covered his eyes to block the sun.

"So, I come out here to give you a message."

"Well, give it." I reached out my hand.

"No, don't have one to *give* to you. Just one to tell you."

I rolled my eyes.

"What's the message you'd like to tell me, Chester?"

"The Colonel wants to have a word with you." He saw the surprise on my face. "Now don't get yer dander up just yet. It don't sound like you're in trouble. I think it's about your pa."

"When?" I said. "Where?"

"Today, round four at his house. Said the girls are gonna be gone then for tea or something at Mrs. Moore's house."

"I don't have any idea what time it is now," I said.

"Well, when I left his house, his clock said one o'clock."

"How long ago was that?"

"Well, I walked to my house first."

"So, ten minutes give or take."

"Maybe a little longer, cause I wasn't in no hurry."

"Okay, let's say fifteen minutes. Did you stop at your house?" I asked.

"Yeah. I had some hard tack and Pa made me clean out the crapper."

"So how long do you think that took?

"An hour, maybe an hour and a half."

"Then what?"

"I came here." Chester kicked at the dirt.

"Did you walk or did you run?"

"Little of both. Mostly walked."

"Any dilly dallying on the way?"

"Nah, not really."

"So, another fifteen minutes of walking?"

"I did stop one time to water the bushes."

"Jingo, Chester! I don't know what to make of you sometimes. Let's say it took you twenty minutes to walk here, and we've wasted another five minutes tryin' to figure out how much time I have before I need to git. According to my figurin' it's probably after three o'clock by now."

He drew circles in the dirt with the toe of his boot. "Sounds 'bout right."

"I guess I better be gittin' then. You comin' along?" I said.

"Yeah, I'll walk with you to my house."

Chester looked down the road. "You better keep to the crick and the woods from here on out," Chester said as we parted ways in front of his property. I did as he'd suggested so as not to be spied by angry adults.

I knocked on the back door of the McEwen house. My knuckles against the glass sounded weak, barely able to penetrate the house. A towhee sang "drink your tea" from the branches above the meat house. I knocked again a little harder.

A voice came from out of nowhere. "He said to go on in." I half jumped out of my skin. It was Mammy. She had been tending to the flower garden.

"Hi, Mammy."

"Long time no see, Vitus. Hear yous been in a might a trouble."

I gave a gentle nod. "I better go on in," I said as I grabbed the knob.

"You got any news 'bout the Union boys?"

"No," I said.

"Rumor got it they's gonna be a big ole fight here in our very Franklin."

"Okay." I opened the door into the expansive kitchen and closed the door behind me, blocking out the conversations of songbirds. The house was quiet as a grave. It smelled like baked bread and candle wax. The grandfather clock ticked from an interior room.

I walked slowly to the entrance of the library, my sweaty bare feet sticky on the floor. The double doors were open.

"Come on in, Vitus," the Colonel said from somewhere inside. He was at his desk writing when I stepped through the threshold.

"Sit down, son."

I sat in the leather chair by his desk that I used to sit in when he'd invite Chester and me in for a debriefing. My palms were sweating. I swallowed hard. The family portrait hung above the fireplace. His son Richard was still a part of the family. Addie must have been four or five years old. She sat on the Colonel's lap in a white dress.

"It has been some time, hasn't it my dear boy?"

"Yes, sir."

"You know that boy will probably never walk again?" He referred to McKlusky. "And his mental faculties have been retarded."

I didn't respond.

"But I didn't bring you here to talk about what you did to those boys, egregious as it was. I have, however, brought you here to talk about your pa."

My heart began to gallop.

"I've been to Hiram Lodge to talk to the provost

marshal about your pa's situation. Long story short, there's nothing I can do to help."

Tears welled in my lids. My eyes burned.

"Son, there's no easy way to tell you this, but… they're going to hang your pa."

My head fell into my hands where I let it all out. Tears and sobs flowed from me for several minutes uninterrupted. The Colonel rose from his chair and walked over beside me. He laid his hand on my shoulder and let me come apart. Eventually, I began to recover. "When?" I wiped the snot and tears on my sleeve.

"First light."

"First light, when?"

"Tomorrow."

Sobs overtook me again.

"Can I see him?"

"Unfortunately son, it's impossible."

"It's not fair, Colonel. First my brother, now my pa."

He rubbed my back.

"They're doing it at the courthouse." His voice was calm.

"Why there? Where everyone can see?"

"To make an example of him, I guess. I'm real sorry son. I promise to be there when it's done to make sure he sees a friendly face, and to step in if they mistreat him."

"Much obliged, sir."

"I did speak on your behalf and the provost marshal agreed to have your pa's body placed in a casket and delivered to your home where you can give him a proper burial. It's the best I could do."

I sniffled and nodded acknowledgement.

"You best be getting home to your ma. Take care of her, Vitus."

I got up to leave. "Thanks for trying, Mr. McEwen."

"Let me know if there is anything you and your ma need. We'll be praying for you."

I walked all the way home, head bowed, kicking stones. I didn't care if anyone saw me.

EIGHTEEN

It was too hot inside the barn, so I spent the night under the maple tree with Thoreau. In the pre-dawn hours, rain began to fall, waking me from a fitful sleep. I moved Thoreau to the barn to get him out of the rain. Overwhelmed by a sense of unfounded energy, I stretched my legs a little and began running toward town in the dark. I had almost memorized every blind step between my barn and the McEwen house.

Men on patrol were taking shelter from the rain and guards slept on front porches. No one was about. I slipped through the alleys and scaled the back of Mr. Whitton's store. Then I ran across the roof to the front, where I sat against the wall and waited. I don't know what had drawn me there; I guess I wanted to see my pa again before he died.

A puddle formed under me as I sat, feeling the rain smack my scalp and listening to it thump my shoulders and trousers. A dog barked from the south. I contemplated the situation in which I had found myself. Why had I come? I didn't want to watch my pa die, but I wanted to see him one last time. Maybe I wanted closure. A part of me hoped he would see me and take comfort in knowing I was okay. That I was independent.

The sun had risen behind dark clouds and no one had yet entered the square. The rain continued to pour until midmorning, when it slowed to a drizzle. A rooster crowed and moments later there were voices in the streets below. I kneeled in the tar of the roof, resting my chin on my arms atop the wall.

Crowds slowly began to form in the square, a mix of blue jackets, dark dresses, and overcoats. The ladies were under umbrellas, the men under hats. The general attitude of the assembly was subdued, melancholy. Conversations were whispered, yet I could make out a few words.

The Colonel walked down Main Street and made his way to the corner of the square and stood in front of the courthouse. It was a bit of a comfort seeing him there, keeping his promise to care for Pa.

A column of bluecoats formed from the courthouse to the opposite side of the square, where Pa came into view. Three Yankees were prodding him along. I studied their faces, memorizing distinguishing features. Pa's hands were bound and he was nearly doubled over. His limp, his familiar limp, had become much more labored. His clothes were tattered and stained with blood. His face was pale and thin. His cheek bones stabbed outward and his eyes appeared sunken and dark.

They marched him up the steps of the courthouse between the huge iron columns, under the noose that hung from the railing of the balcony above. They escorted him inside. A few minutes later they emerged on the balcony.

Standing at the railing, Pa looked down at the crowd as the provost marshal spouted off some legal manure. He panned across the faces, probably looking for mine or Ma's. I stood and waved my arms back and forth.

The hangman placed the noose around his neck and asked if he wanted to be blindfolded or not. He chose the latter. They forced him over the railing and to stand on the small ledge. I jumped up and down waving my arms again. Without thinking, I yelled out, "Pa!"

The crowd turned toward me and Pa looked up. We made eye contact. A big smile stretched across his dirty face.

"It'll be okay, son!" His voice echoed through the square. Sounds of mumbling came from the crowd.

"Take care of your ma," he said as they tightened the noose. "I'll be with James." They tried to push him off, but he managed to grab the railing with his fingers despite the bindings on his wrist. The crowd gasped. The hangman pried Pa's fingers.

"Don't let these Invaders—"

Pa fell.

A horrifying crack split the air as the rope jerked taut. The crowd screamed and diverted their eyes. His body swung violently under the balcony, almost reaching the ceiling of the porch. The railing flexed in and out. I couldn't take my eyes off the spectacle.

The square became deathly quiet, only a soft hiss from the falling mist. The rope squeaked and groaned under Pa's weight. His swinging was almost hypnotic, surreal.

Surely that wasn't my pa swinging like a clock pendulum between the columns above the courthouse steps. The courthouse the Colonel himself helped design and build five years before.

His body continued hanging over the steps, an Invader ducked under his feet as he exited the courthouse. I had seen enough.

Tears and rain blurring my vision, I climbed down into the alley. Before I could make it through a pile of trash, I was grabbed from behind in a crushing bear hug and lifted from the ground.

Thrashing violently, I swung my elbows backward at his head and kicked my heels into his crotch. An elbow clipped his jaw. With a grunt, he dropped me. I turned to lay eyes on my attacker. It was McKlusky's father. His hand on his jaw. His eyes glowing with fury. Without thinking, I gave him a pushing kick in the stomach sending him stumbling into a heap of garbage.

I looked down on him, ready to spring on him and finish him off, but I felt a bit of pity. I had no qualms with this man. I couldn't blame him. My pa would have done the same if the tables had been turned. I left him there in the trash and ran home, whimpering the whole way.

The house was still. The air was heavy and dank like a mausoleum. The sheen curtains danced slightly in front of the open window in the kitchen. The washbasin and floor were wet with rainwater. Ma was awake but unmoving in her bed. The smell in the room was a mix of the rainy outdoors and stale urine.

A yellowish brown stain had blossomed on the quilt near her legs. Her blank eyes stared through the open window at the sugar maple, ignoring the intrusion of rain. The wall under the sill shined with moisture, puddles gathered on the floorboards.

I kissed her on the forehead and stroked her hair. I whispered, "I love you, Ma," then closed the window and retreated to the kitchen where I lay on a bench and dozed off.

In the late afternoon, I awoke to the squeak of wagon wheels and the beat of hooves. A Yankee on horseback pulled a simple wagon containing Pa's pine coffin. Behind him was the entire McEwen family and Chester. The Yankee and the wagon waited on the road while the others enveloped me in hugs, tears flowing. Mrs. McEwen, carrying a large basket, led the girls to the house. They were all dressed in black. Addie and I made eye contact. Her sweet face showed love and sympathy. I was slightly embarrassed by my vulnerability.

"It's a tough thing to have to decide, son," the Colonel said. "But have you given any thought to where you'd like your father to rest?"

I thought it over a minute and pointed at the maple tree. "Over there, I guess."

The Colonel directed the Yankee to take the coffin under the tree, where he unceremoniously dragged it off the wagon. The coffin hit the ground hard with a thunk. He pulled two shovels from the back and tossed them on the ground.

As he climbed back on his horse, a muffled whinny came from the barn. Thoreau. The man turned toward the barn, then back at me. Even through my vision was blurred by tears, I recognized him right away. The man with the birthmark. My head swelled with an animal rage.

He gave me a menacing look. A look that said he knew I had a horse that didn't belong to me. His glare told me he'd be back another day to confiscate it and to hang me. String me up in a noose like my father. But for something less noble, for horse thievery. He clicked at his new horse and set it walking toward town.

For a fleeting moment, fear trumped depression. When the man with the birthmark disappeared over the rise, my heart slowed and returned to melancholia.

Chester, the Colonel, and I spent the next couple hours digging Pa's grave. The sky cleared an hour or so before dusk. The sun, low on the horizon ushered the rain away, leaving it hot and muggy. The leaves of the sugar maple filtered its light on our backs as we shoveled the soft dirt in silence.

When we finished, the Colonel escorted the ladies from the house. They had somehow washed Ma and dressed her in a black funeral gown. She was emaciated and could hardly walk under her own power. The team of girls practically dragged her across the dooryard to the burial site. The Colonel followed with a small wood chair from the house.

Chester came from the barn with rope that we tied to each side of the coffin. He and I on one side, the Colonel on the other, we lowered Pa into the cool, dark hole. I blinked away tears as the Colonel said a few words and a prayer. Ma, made no sound, just stared. Mrs. McEwen held her upright.

Chester and I shoveled dirt onto the pine box. Each thud of dirt on the lid was like someone boxing my ears. When we finished, we all helped carry Ma back in the house. The McEwen girls had cleaned the place up and replaced Ma's bed sheets. Tears welled behind my lids at the show of such compassion. It took everything I had not to dissolve into a blubbering mess. But I was now man of the house. I had responsibilities. I had to be strong for Ma.

Very few words were exchanged the whole time everyone was there. Mostly just soft touches on my back and downcast faces. In the waning daylight, everyone started home. Addie hugged me tightly. I didn't want to let go. Mrs. McEwen left me gingerbread cookies and bacon.

I slept in the bed beside Ma that night. Short nightmares flashed episodically all night. Images of Pa swinging between the columns of the courthouse. Only instead of thirty feet tall and six feet around, the columns grew to ten times their size. Pa's body only a tiny dark line dangling like an insect in a gargantuan spider's web.

McKlusky's pa lifting me in a bear hug flashed before me. This time I was too slow to defend myself. He squeezed me so hard, I helplessly watched the lower half of my body separate and fall to the ground.

A sinister voice echoed through my dreamscape. It belonged to the Yankee with the birthmark. He laughed maniacally and said he was coming back to take Thoreau and burn the house down with Ma and me in it. His laugh morphed into the caw of a crow. I woke up drenched in sweat. A murder of crows had gathered around Pa's grave, picking at the freshly turned soil.

NINETEEN

I had become very anxious about Thoreau's safety. Birthmark and others would come for him and they'd wreak havoc on our fields too. After eating Mrs. McEwen's bacon, I rode Thoreau across the fields into the forest where two hills converged that Chester and I had named Dead Goat Hollow. A few summers back, we had tracked a stray goat and found it dead in the stream that ran through the bottom. The goat was stuck in mud and was too heavy to move. So we left it there to rot. It took two years to decay.

I found a spot where a large oak had fallen in years past making an opening in the canopy where a patch of grass and shrubs could grow. I let Thoreau graze while I built a horse-size arbor out of beech and pine branches beside a small stream.

Then, I created a large encirclement with a makeshift fence I made by jamming branches and logs horizontally into forks of trees and shrubs. I built the camp in a rush, but it would be just enough to keep Thoreau in one spot.

I found some crab apples and made a little pile under the shelter. I lay my forehead on the lightning bolt blaze and rubbed his big cheeks. "You'll be safe here, ole buddy," I told him. "I need to go home and check on Ma, but I'll be back first thing in the morning." He shook his head to shoo a fly that had been drinking from his eye.

THE NEXT TWO DAYS I VISITED THOREAU AND TOOK HIM FOR rides, careful to stay away from open fields. At night, I stayed in the house with Ma, Excalibur and the Whitworth by my side. I expected the Yankees any day. It was an overcast morning when they finally showed up.

I was coming back to the house after picking a basketful of green beans, when movement on the road caught my eye. It was three men dressed in blue. I ran into the house where I was unsuccessful at rousing Ma. I strapped Excalibur to my back and grabbed the Whitworth. Intense heat growing behind my face, I walked up the road to meet them.

"Halt!" I said.

"Whoa, there partner," the man with the birthmark said. "There's no need to point that thing at us."

I had the Whitworth trained on his chest. He was empty-handed, but had a sidearm strapped to his waist. The man on his left was carrying a rifle, and the other man also had a pistol in its holster.

"You're trespassin'!" I yelled. "You have no right to be here! State your business!"

"I think you know our business, son," Birthmark said.

"Don't call me son!"

They continued toward me, hands out in front of them as if approaching an ornery horse.

"We ain't goin' to hurt you or your mom. Just let us take a quick inventory and we'll be on our way."

"One more step, and I'll put a hole in your chest." My temper boiled.

"You only get one shot, son. That leaves two more of us. Then what?"

"It won't matter to you, cause you'll be in hell." I shook the end of the barrel at him.

"Look at him," the one with the rifle said. "He can barely hold that thing up!"

"I'm warning you!"

They were within ten paces of me. I took a step backward, feeling like a wild animal defending my young. They didn't stop their approach. The man began to raise his rifle. The next ten to fifteen seconds were a blur.

I aimed the Whitworth at the man with the rifle and fired. Before he hit the ground I had thrown the Whitworth down, drawn Excalibur and sprung toward them. Taking advantage of their visible bewilderment, I had closed the distance before the other two could draw their pistols.

Excalibur laid open a gash on one man's forehead and shattered his nose. As he reeled backward, I struck the man with the birthmark on the wrist as he reached for his pistol, a sickening crack indicated breaking bones. A second stroke of my sword clipped a small chunk off the tip of his nose. He fell to the ground hollering.

I turned toward the other man, who was attempting to

staunch the flow of blood as he tried to stand. He was in a state of shock, visibly shaken.

"Go ahead," I yelled. "Try and grab your pistol!"

He stumbled a little and lowered one hand from his face toward the gun. In a flash, Excalibur broke his hand. On the return stroke, the wooden blade of my sword found the side of his head.

His body fell into the dirt with a thud and didn't move again. My chest heaved and my pulse pounded in my head as I looked down on my evil work. Seconds passed before I realized the man with the birthmark had fled. He was disappearing over a rise.

I ran after him. By the time I had overtaken the hill, he was nowhere to be seen. I spent the better part of a half hour hunting him before I gave up. I had to deal with the two bodies before anyone passed by.

Upon seeing the lifeless men lying on the road in their blue jackets and shiny decorations, I suddenly felt sick and vomited in the grass. I was overcome with an odd mix of regret, fear, and contempt. I was still only a boy and had ended the life of two men.

I sat in the road staring at their bodies until I could convince myself that what I had done was justified. These were the people responsible for my brother's death, my father's death, and the destruction of my town. They had come to steal my horse and harm Ma and me. It was either them or me.

Fear became the overpowering force. I was a murderer. I was in a lot of trouble. I dragged the bodies, one at a time, into a nearby bog where I buried them in shallow graves and covered them with brush. I then kicked dirt over the blood stains in the road. I kept their firearms and ammunition and hid them in the barn.

By the time I had gone into the house, the full gravity of the situation hit me. Seeing Ma lying helpless on the mattress suddenly made me realize the kind of trouble I was in. We couldn't stay. The birthmark man would surely alert the rest of the Yankees. A blue mob would soon be overtaking our land seeking justice. I had to get Ma out of there.

Faster than my feet had ever taken me, I ran through rows of corn and soybeans to Dead Goat Hollow to retrieve Thoreau. We rode hard back to the farm where I set straight to work. I tore the barn door off and nailed it to two pieces split rails from Pa's unfinished fence. I tied the whole contraption to Thoreau's saddle. I then dragged the mattress from my bed and tied it down to the door.

Ma still hadn't moved. I slid my arms under her legs and shoulders to lift her. Her body had withered to skin and bones, a light load. I carried her outside and lay her on the makeshift travois. She was still in her black gown. She laid her arm over her eyes to block the glare, but that was her only movement. There were no protests from her. No questions.

I covered her with blankets and gently tied her to the barn door. Thoreau dragged the door behind as we slowly trekked around the fields to the camp. After I got her situated under the shelter, Thoreau and I set off to the farm with the barn door travois in tow.

I gathered some kitchen utensils, a few articles of Ma's

clothes, the fox skin I'd given her for Christmas, candles, and any food we had. I piled anything and everything we might need on the door. I tucked *Daniel Boone* and *Robinson Crusoe* and the Colonel's field glasses in the saddle bag and secured my two rifles, pistol, and sword. I stuffed oats in a feed bag and hay in two other bags.

Twice on the way back to the camp, we had to stop so I could retrieve fallen items, <u>but we eventually made it. With Thoreau and Ma safe,</u> I took a couple empty bags back to our fields and collected as much corn and beans as I could.

I spent the rest of the day building a separate lean-to for Ma and me. When I was done and had moved her inside, I built a fire and boiled some beans and corn in a pot.

"How does this suit ya, Ma?" Her back was to me, still unresponsive. I ate the vegetables while Thoreau crunched on his oats.

I lay on a quilt beside Ma and watched as the forest filled with the flashes of fireflies. The peaceful gurgling of the stream was soon drowned out by the arguments of the katydids, *Katy did, Katy didn't. Katy did, Katy didn't.* Mosquitoes buzzed in my ears and Thoreau thumped around near his shelter. Curled up with my back against Ma, I watched my small campfire fade to embers as I dozed off into a world of nightmares. Pools of blood on the dirt road. The blast of gunfire. The shrieks of men being dragged out of this world into hell. Chasing the man with the birthmark, only my legs were heavy as lead. The gory face that was once McKlusky's. Addie's scream.

. . .

At dawn, I bid Ma a good morning and told her what I had planned for the day. I might as well have been talking to a log. I took Excalibur and the Whitworth back to the farm. To stay discreet, I left Thoreau at camp. I kneeled at the edge of the cornfield and used the field glasses to see if there was any movement near the house. Satisfied there wasn't anyone around, I approached with caution.

ma still not answering

Finding the house and barn free of intruders, I searched for anything else I might have missed. Ma's black cloak hung on the back of the chair. I grabbed that and a couple of knives and cups, and shoved them in a canvas messenger bag.

It was creepy being alone at our farm. Ma hadn't been much company as of late, but her absence was felt. I leaned against the basin as the dry heat sucked sweat from my face and the droning of the cicadas rang in my ears. The table in the kitchen brought to mind dinners with Pa, Ma, and James. We'd never do it again. Nothing would ever be the same. I whimpered a little, the tears feeling cool on my face.

I stepped into the breezy, fresh air, under a bank of fluffy clouds temporarily hiding the sun. Its shadow slid over the barn into the fields. I had a heavy feeling I was being watched by more than the whirring cicadas. I jogged until I was concealed between rows of corn. I looked back at the small house, the big barn, and the old sugar maple marking Pa's grave. Something inside felt like I was saying farewell forever.

On my walk back to camp, I considered what to do with Ma. Should I take her somewhere for help? Where would I go? Could she even survive a trip on the back of a sled in the summer heat? An idea finally struck me when I was heating some pine needle tea that evening.

Ma and Pa had friends outside city limits that may be able to help her. They would be far enough from town the Yankees wouldn't bother them. I had been there once. They called the house The Meeting of the Waters because the Big Harpeth River and the West Harpeth converged on their property. Ma and Pa took James and me there when I was young to have lunch and visit their horse farm.

Unfortunately, I remembered the ride in a wagon taking more than an hour on roads. There were also a couple river crossings. I didn't even know if the bridges were still there. Fording a river with Ma would prove difficult. I didn't have much choice. She couldn't lie in the forest. She needed help.

I lay beside her again that night. She never moved. Her breathing was weak and irregular. A heavy fog bank descended into the valley overnight and brought with it a damp chill.

At dawn, the forest was a light gray. Obscured shapes of trees filtered through the murk, and the dark form of Thoreau was beside the stream. I threw a pile of sticks on the mound of ashes and stoked the coals into a fire. After placing a few small logs on top, I ventured into the mist to find more firewood.

Visibility was limited and the axe I had brought was dull, so it took longer than I had anticipated. I was famished by the time I returned. I brought water to boil and cooked more beans and corn.

After breakfast, I brushed Thoreau and practiced my sword fighting until the sun burned off the fog. I wanted to give Thoreau some exercise, so I saddled him and walked him out of the forest, where we trotted on the edges of fields to the west. On the way back I noticed another bank of fog moving across the field that separated camp from the farm. It was moving in our direction. On the breeze, I could smell smoke. Something about it made my blood turn cold.

We galloped toward home until we were choking on smoke and decided it best to turn back. I tied Thoreau to a bush at the edge of the forest and made my way back. The cornfield was consumed in a thick white smoke. Stagnant and heavy. I felt my way through the stalks, my eyes burning. As I neared the edge, hell stood before me.

Towers of orange flames shot into the air where my house and barn stood. I stifled a scream for fear the Invaders were still around. I fell into the dirt sobbing. The feeling of loss, hopelessness, and fury, all at once overcame me. I stormed back through the corn, knocking down stalks like an angry giant in a forest. By the time I reached Thoreau, a light rain had started falling. As I secured him under his arbor, a clap of thunder signaled the start of a storm. It came hard and fast. The tops of the trees danced back and forth overhead and the rain came in torrents.

The rain would help stymie the fire, but I feared it wouldn't be enough. I sat under my lean-to cleaning the Whitworth. I packed the powder and tapped the hexagonal bullet down the barrel with the ramrod. I cocked the hammer, and placed a cap on the nipple and gently eased the hammer back down.

I sat for fifteen minutes or so, seething, until the rain slowed to a drizzle. I was so hellbent on revenge, I didn't even check on Ma before I started running through the woods like a deer then across the fields until I was in shooting range of the house. I paused and used the field glasses. The house was a black shell—small fires still flickered in the drizzle and thick plumes of smoke poured from within. The barn was nothing more than a smoldering pile. I couldn't see anyone moving.

I approached cautiously with the Whitworth cocked and at the ready. The charred remains of the structures crackled and hissed. No one was around. A section of the house groaned in a light wind. The heat from the smoldering remains irritated my arms and face. I sat in the grass, arms across my knees, and stared at the ruins of my house. A thin tendril of smoke drifted from a pile of black timber where Thoreau's stall would have been.

Droplets of mist gathered on my eyelashes and mixed with tears when I blinked. As I sat in the wet grass, a hot fury replaced an empty sorrow inside of me. I made a vow to myself that I would kill the man with the birthmark. I would take Ma to the Meeting of the Waters where she'd be safe and I'd then hunt him down.

MA LAY IN A FETAL POSITION LIKE SHE HAD SINCE THE morning before. I didn't bother telling her about the house. I didn't know if she'd ever get back there, so there was no use in upsetting her further. Her condition, brought on by the deaths of my brother and father, would only worsen. I poked at the fire and talked to Ma about the progress of the crops and told her the plan to visit the Perkinses and that we'd leave in the morning. As I had expected, Ma gave no response.

The next morning, I was in a hurry to get moving. Instead of rekindling the fire, I tied the barn door sled to Thoreau in preparation for Ma's transport. I gave Ma a gentle nudge on the shoulder to let her know I was going to move her to the sled. When she did not respond, I gave her a little shake.

Her body didn't react with the swaying of a pliable living being, but rocked back and forth stiffly. "Ma!" I shook her again, her thin muscled arms felt like wood. Her face was pale and her lips a deep purple. A fly crawled from her nose and took flight. "Ma!" I cried out, shaking her more violently. "No! You can't leave me too!" I buried my face in her arm, her sleeve soaking up my tears.

I don't know how long I lay there sobbing, but when I eventually cried myself out, dusk was near and an owl hooted from the hillside to my left. Another replied from my right. I covered Ma's head with her quilt. Then I untied the sled from Thoreau and boiled some corn. I dragged my quilts under Thoreau's arbor where I eventually dozed off.

Buzzing mosquitoes roused me at dawn. The rain had stopped and songbirds were conversing. I had no appetite and decided against fooling with a fire. Instead, I tied the travois back on Thoreau, scooped up Ma and her mattress, secured them to barn door, and headed home.

ONE OF THE SHOVELS WE USED FOR PA'S GRAVE WAS STILL leaning against the maple. Beside it a piece of paper had been nailed into the scaly bark between long-healed bore holes we'd made for syrup taps. WANTED it said in large print at the top. Underneath was "Dead or Alive," and a poorly drawn likeness of me. The bottom quarter of the page read "$200 REWARD for the capture of one Vitus Swinggate."

A week before, I would have been crippled with fear at seeing this sign. But now, it didn't faze me. I ripped it off the tree and found a patch of hot ashes in our house rubble where I poked it in with a stick, setting it on fire.

It took me most of the day to dig Ma's grave beside Pa's. The rain had brought in cooler temperatures and clear skies. A gentle wind swished through the crown of the maple. Leaves on the branches closest to the house, browned and crispy from the heat of the fire, rustled like hundreds of tiny bones clinking together.

The hole was waist deep when I stood in it, reaching over the fresh dirt to Ma's body. She felt light as I pulled her to me, gathering her in my arms. I carefully set her body down in the grave. After covering her up, I leaned on the shovel handle waiting for the tears to come, but they never did. I felt I hadn't any left. I had cried my limit, which bothered me. I was afraid I was exhibiting similar symptoms as Ma. Was I going to die of a broken heart too?

"Goodbye, Ma," I said.

A gust of wind gushed through the canopy of the maple in response. The entire tree swayed, branches swinging independently, leaves whistling. I imagined it was Ma's soul going to heaven to be with James and Pa. She abandoned me to be with the God who seemed to have abandoned her.

I had no one left but my horse and nowhere to live.

Who would blame me for contracting the sorrow sickness after all I had lost. The remains of Pa's fence poked above the grass. His voice entered my head. *Don't let these Invaders—* he had cried out as he was pushed from the courthouse balcony. That's when I decided I would not die of a broken heart. I'd have my revenge on the Invaders. And I'd start with the man with the birthmark.

he is determined to get his revenge.

TWENTY

Thoreau and I stayed at our camp in the ravine west of our home for a few days. I mostly used crops from our farm to keep us fed and snag trees I could push over for firewood. I had spent some time bolstering the shelters to provide more warmth from the approaching autumn nights. Staying busy was the key to taking my mind off the recent atrocities. When not focused on a task at hand, much of my thinking centered around my plan for revenge.

A GRAY AND GLOOMY DAWN FOUND ME HUDDLED TIGHTLY under my quilt. An unseasonably cold air had settled in the valley. The forest was silent, save for the trickling of the stream and a solitary frog. Then voices.

I threw off the quilt, grabbed my pistol and ran to the edge of the field. I crouched behind a screen of blackberry bushes. Dozens of men in gray picked through our fields.

A Rebel foraging party. Frozen with fear, I watched as they wiped out most of our crops like a swarm of locusts.

I knew then that it was time to move. I had to get Thoreau to the Meeting of the Waters horse farm. The encounter was too close for comfort. Gray or Blue, if they would have found me, they would have taken Thoreau and my weapons. And lord knows what they would have done to me.

After a small breakfast, I found a beech tree up the hill from camp that had a hollowed-out bottom. It was large enough to store all of my belongings. I kept Excalibur on my back and the pistol tucked in my belt.

We walked past my farm and headed north. The fields were mostly barren and the forests were less dense than those on the hills. The trees were larger and more spread out. The understory was mostly grass and briars. We crossed two creeks before finding the West Harpeth River. The only route I knew was to follow the river until it met with the Big Harpeth. At the confluence is where I'd find the Perkinses' Meeting of the Waters house. It was not the quickest route, but it was less likely I'd get lost.

Nearing dusk, the river intersected a small road. A modest bridge I recognized from my youth crossed the water. The Perkins's property was just beyond. I hid Excalibur and my pistol in the crotch of an old Osage orange trunk.

Mrs. Perkins greeted me with guarded hospitality at the front steps. It was clear she had heard about my brother and Pa, but had also learned of my status as a wanted outlaw. Looking around the property behind me, she ushered me inside.

"We're sorry for your loss, Vitus." Mrs. Perkins invited me to sit in the parlor.

"Thank you, ma'am."

"What can we do for you?" Anxiety showed in her face.

"Well," I stammered, "I was hoping you could help me."

Mr. Perkins and her daughters talked noisily in the kitchen.

"And how can we do that, Vitus? We are well aware you are wanted for murder."

"Yes, ma'am, but—"

"It's a crime for me to have you inside my house."

"Yes, ma'am. I understand. I'm not staying. I was just hoping you would keep my horse."

"Keep your horse?"

"Yes ma'am, I'm afraid the Yankee Invaders will take him. I'd feel much better knowing he was here with you all."

Mr. Perkins entered the parlor, his daughters, like ducklings filed in behind him.

"What's going on in here?"

"He wants to board his horse here," Mrs. Perkins said.

"No, ma'am, you all can keep him."

"Where are you going, son?" Mr. Perkins said. "And where's your mother?"

I told them about the Invaders burning down our house and Ma dying of a broken heart. I explained how I killed the men on the road in self-defense. I didn't tell them I had been plotting a killing spree. Instead, I just told them I was going to travel around and maybe find the Army of Tennessee and enlist.

Mr. and Mrs. Perkins looked at each other. "We can take on another horse," Mr. Perkins said.

Mrs. Perkins, feeling sympathy for me, touched my cheek. "Sweetie, I wish we could keep you here too, but—"

"No, ma'am," I interrupted. "It would be too dangerous for your family, but thank you."

Mr. Perkins put his hand on my shoulder. "Well it's almost dark. You can sup with us and sleep in the barn tonight. In the morning, you can be off."

"Oh, Thomas, he can stay in the house one night, can't he?"

"No, ma'am," I said before Mr. Perkins could answer. "If it's all the same to you, I'd rather sleep in the barn with Thoreau. It's what I did at home anyway."

"Thoreau?" they both said.

"Yes, ma'am, sir. I named him after Henry David Thoreau, the writer."

"Good name," Mr. Perkins said.

AFTER DINNER, MR. PERKINS SHOWED THOREAU AND ME TO A large horse barn behind the house. There were a dozen or more stalls, all filled with horses except for one on the end they were using to store tack.

"We can move this out tonight," Mr. Perkins said. "Maybe in the morning you can help me move it to the loft."

"Yes, sir. Gladly, sir."

We piled saddles, ropes, halters, and straw bales in the center of the barn and lined the stall with fresh straw.

"You gonna be all right out here, son?" he said as he ruffled my hair.

"Yes, sir. Thank you."

He left a lantern hanging between two stalls and closed the barn doors behind him. I lay on the floor, using a saddle as a pillow and a horse blanket as a quilt. Thoreau was safely tucked away in his stall. The swollen river rushed below. The water of the West Harpeth flowing over boulders and colliding with the Big Harpeth. Henry David Thoreau once said, "He who hears the rippling of water, will not utterly despair of anything." I took comfort knowing my friend would hear the rippling every night. The river's hypnotic melody, mixed with sounds of horses stomping in straw and tails swishing, lulled me to sleep.

I had moved most of the tack up to the loft before the first rooster crowed. Mrs. Perkins brought me a loaf of bread for breakfast just as I was finishing. The whole Perkins family came out to the barn to move the horses to the field. I hugged Thoreau's neck tightly and kissed the white lightning bolt on his face.

"You'll be happy here, boy. You'll be safe and you can run with the other horses. You don't have to live in a crumby shelter in the forest with the likes of me."

Tears welled, but never flowed, saving face with the Perkins girls.

I rubbed his ears and told him I'd come back and visit. He trotted off with the other horses. I thanked the Perkins family and they bid me farewell. Just before I rounded a bend, I looked back. In the middle of the meadow, with the other horses galloping in a circle, Thoreau was rolling around in the grass and sliding on his back. He was far off, but I bet there was a smile on his face.

I retrieved my weapons and followed the river south. After an hour of walking, I stopped to eat some bread. The sun was high above, perceptively farther south than its path had been when we planted the crops.

A great blue heron stood knee deep in the river, staring patiently at the water. He was still as a statue. I slowly lowered myself onto a log and tore off a bite of bread, watching. Without warning, the heron stabbed his head into the water and came back up with no reward. He shook the water from his head, then acted as if he had just noticed me. He eyed me for a minute, turning his head back and forth.

I contemplated my new life of solitude while the heron ignored me and inched back and forth looking for prey. Like him, I was a loner who had to survive in the wild. I didn't need anyone. He struck the water again. This time yanking out a small fish and throwing his head back to swallow it. We were both killers out of necessity, but unlike the heron, I would not only stalk prey to eat, but I'd also have to kill for justice. A concept my bird friend wouldn't understand.

When I finally stood to leave, the heron took off with large, labored strokes and sailed silently above the water, following the curves of the river. I picked myself up and followed his lead. An hour later I was almost back to my new home.

Pistol at the ready, I cautiously approached camp from the hill above. It looked unoccupied as I had expected. The adjacent fields were empty. Everything seemed copacetic. I started a new fire and retrieved my things from the beech tree. I laid out the quilt and rifles under my shelter and made a wild onion broth.

As I stared at flames rolling around inside a hollow log, I realized I had become Daniel Boone and Robinson Crusoe. I wasn't on an island, but I was isolated and living off the land. Instead of cannibals and Shawnee Indians, I had to fend off Yankees.

The fire popped, then hissed. The trickle of the stream somehow sounded sad because Thoreau wasn't stomping around beside it. I found *Daniel Boone* and *Robinson Crusoe* and a candle in the feedbag. I chose to read about Crusoe's island on the other side of the world until I fell asleep on a bed of pine needles.

In the middle of the night, I abruptly awoke to a scream. It sounded like a witch. A witch? Could I have heard a witch? The sound was distinct and nearby. I was paralyzed and numb. The forest became silent again.

I had heard tales of witches but hadn't believed them. Could there be a witch in Dead Goat Hollow? Stalking me? Did she come to punish me for the murders? Was she an agent of the devil, here to take me to hell?

Other than my heart pounding in my head, I could only hear the faint sound of dew dripping from the leaves and the gurgle of the stream. Shivering now from fear and cold, I pulled the quilt over my face and listened for the witch to make her approach. A small cracking sound came from behind the shelter several yards off.

Very slowly, I pulled the pistol to my chest. The fire pit only contained a thin red glow. I flinched when an owl hooted from the darkness above me. Stillness. Another hoot. I tried to reason with myself that if a witch was in the vicinity, the owl would have flown off. I used that justification to slow my breathing and calm down. After several minutes of silence, I assumed the witch was gone. The owl continued hooting periodically, conversing with another near the top of the hill.

My mind was restless the balance of the night. I tossed and turned under the quilt. Being alone was harder than I'd thought. At some point I dozed off and found myself in a dream. I was sleeping in the barn above Thoreau and for whatever reason, Ma and Addie were outside knocking on the boards of the barn, calling my name. Their knocks grew louder and louder.

I became conscious again, aware of the forest around me. Ma and Addie's knocks still resonating in my ears. The knocks continued as clearly as two knuckles wrapping on a door. I opened my eyes, the branches above slightly swaying. Knock, knock, knock. I sat up. No one was around. Where Thoreau used to stand, there was only an area of grass and leaf debris that had been tamped down by his hooves.

Knock, knock, knock.

Out of my daze now, I realized I was hearing a woodpecker. When I stood to stretch my back, it flew off showing its disapproval with a piercing call that sounded like an old lady laughing.

I had figured solitude would be a lonely affair, but clearly it was going to be scary for a while. I just hoped I'd get accustomed to the sounds of the forest soon.

For the first half of the day I did nothing more than mollygrubbing. I became bored quickly. I had decided to visit Chester that night, and the time until then seemed to crawl by like an injured slug. I walked the crop fields, finding bits and pieces of edible vegetables. What the graybacks didn't take, the crows helped themselves to.

I gathered a handful of dandelions and the roots of a Queen Anne's lace. Back at camp, I ate a bitter salad and drank from the stream. I lay in the grass where Thoreau once stood and read more of Crusoe's adventures. When the sun was finally low on the horizon, I started off in a jog toward town carrying the pistol and Excalibur. I ran past the tangled black remains of my house, skirted the forest edge, and passed through rows of dead corn and the beds of creeks.

Chester's house was dark. A dog barked to the east. I tapped on his window, setting off a series of bumps and racket mixed with swearing. It was his pa, and he was mad as a rattlesnake. I dove behind the old wagon just before he threw the door open, shotgun on his shoulder.

"Who's there!" he yelled into the empty darkness. "I know someone's there. Show ye self." He stumbled around the yard.

Chester's pa was the kind of man who would turn his own son's best friend in for two hundred dollars, so I decided to remain in the grass. After a bit of huffing and puffing, he went back inside and slammed the door. The entire tiny house seemed to shake.

I tip toed back to Chester's window. I figured he was at the McEwen house. I mixed spit and dirt and used it to write a message on the pane. "Dead Goat Hollow, V."

I ran on light feet back to camp, almost giddy about the prospect of seeing my friend soon.

He didn't show up until the next afternoon. I watched through my field glasses as he crossed the fields. As I had hoped he would do, he looked back every so often to make sure he wasn't being followed. I swept the landscape behind him with the glass for the same reason. As he neared the hollow, I made my way down the hill.

I was perched on a fallen tree that cantilevered off the hill. It startled him when he saw me. "You ain't a ghost are ya?" he said as he took another cautious step.

"Nah, not yet." I jumped to the slope and ran down to him. A big smile stretched his cheeks. We both laughed and gave each other a hug.

"How ya doin' pard?" He put his arm around my shoulder. I returned the embrace and steered him toward the shelter.

"Oh, I'm makin' it," I said. I was elated. I hadn't had any quality human contact in a coon's age.

We worked together to collect wood and build a large fire. While we were breaking sticks and pushing down dead trees, he filled me in on the goings on in town. He never asked about Ma or Thoreau. We didn't bring up the murders or Ma until we were eating a mushroom soup we had prepared.

"You're a wanted man, Vitus. But I guess you knew that."

I nodded. He was quiet for a few minutes.

"Do you want to talk about it?" he asked.

"There's not much to say." I pushed a log farther into the fire with my boot.

"I'm real sorry about yer ma. What happened anyway?"

"Broken heart. What are they sayin' around town about it?"

"About yer ma? Nothing really. Not sure very many people know about it. The ones who do have mixed up stories about it. About the whole thing. You know, the murders and all."

"It wasn't murder, it was self-defense."

"Some say the Yankees killed your ma and you avenged her."

"Nah, that ain't how it happened."

"The man who escaped is spreading rumors. I doubt they're true."

"Like what?" I said, my cheeks heating up.

"Said they was just at your farm to help y'all out and that you had gone mad. Claimed you killed your own ma and killed his friends in cold blood to cover for it."

"Oh, that's rich." I threw a rock into the trees.

"He said he barely made it out alive."

"That ain't how it went at all."

"I know that, Vitus, but I don't know what actually happened. I just know that everyone in town is scared of you and all the Yankees are looking for you. They think you're some raving lunatic living in the forest looking for more people to kill."

"Everyone?"

"Well, not me of course. But, yeah, everyone." He took a sip from his cup.

"Even Addie, Vit."

That was a kick in the stomach.

"The McEwens are scared of you and *for* you. They know you've had it rough, but they're of the mind you've gone crazy. Even if you ain't crazy, they know the Yankees are out to get you and see you hanged." He picked at the inside of his cup with his finger trying to fish out a mushroom.

"I hate saying it, Vit, but the Colonel told me and Addie that we were to stay away from you. Said it would only be trouble. The Yankees are gathering search parties for you, and some of the townspeople are after ya too."

The heat of tears gathered behind my lids. I pretended as if smoke had gotten in my eyes and wiped them away with the back of my hand.

"So, I've lost Addie?"

"Fraid so, pard. I'm sorry."

I blinked away a few more tears.

"What should I tell them happened?"

I told him every detail. About the man with the birthmark scowling at me when he brought Pa's casket. About how they came back threatening to take Thoreau and possibly hurt Ma. How the man reached for his gun and I shot in self-defense. I told him how Ma's health declined after James had died. And how she got worse and worse when Pa died.

I told him about hiding in the forest while the Invaders burned our house and barn down, and how Ma had been dead for two days before I even noticed. Tears rolled down his face by the time I got around to telling him about leaving Thoreau at the Perkins's house.

We were both quiet for a while. Each of us staring blankly at the embers, occasionally poking them with a stick.

"What does Addie think?" I felt vulnerable for expressing my concern for her.

"She's tore up real bad. She's definitely taken a shine to you, but now she thinks you're a monster. First with the McKlusky affair, then the double murder. On top of that all the rumors painted an ugly picture of you. At best, you're a wanted outlaw."

I scooted from the fire a little, my feet were baking. "I guess I am a monster."

"What are you gonna do 'bout it?" His eyes were sincere, friendly.

I stood and walked over to my shelter. When I returned I laid my arsenal near the fire. His eyes lit up as I lined up the Whitworth, the carbine I had stolen from the man on the road, the pistol, my hunting knife, and Excalibur.

"You're an outlaw, Vit. How are you going to get anywhere near them?"

"That's where I'll need your help."

He shook his head and waved his hand.

"Oh, I don't know about that. I can't kill nobody. Even for you, Vit."

"No, that's not what I had in mind. You'll be my eyes and ears. I'll do the rest."

He turned it over in his head.

"Where do we start?" he said with a smile.

I grabbed his shoulder. "The man with the birthmark."

TWENTY-ONE

Chester and I lay by the fire. As he lightly snored, I ruminated about how I had become some demon wandering the forests, a killer. Two bodies were in the bog, and several more people in Franklin bore scars and broken bones from engaging me. The more I thought on it, the more I liked the idea. Addie had already denounced me and there was no way to earn back her trust. I was no longer her Sir Lancelot. I was a villain. I might as well become the monster everyone thought I was. I would earn the reputation of a maniac wandering the woods.

Chester stayed a few nights. I really enjoyed the company, but it was not safe for him to be with me. The McEwens were probably looking for him already. I devised a plan and spelled it out for him.

"Go back to the McEwen house. Tell them you had been out looking for me and that I was nowhere to be found. Tell 'em I must have joined the army or that I was in the barn when it burned. Make sure the Colonel tells the provost marshal. Maybe they'll call off the search for me."

"Okay, I'll tell them."

"Then I want you to find out where the man with the birthmark is staying. Follow him around. Get to know his routines. Report back to me. Don't come here, cause I'll be gone. It's too risky for me to stay in one place for long."

"How will I find you?"

"You won't. I'll find you. Remember the tree with the trunk that was all twisted up? We called it Twisting Tree?"

"Yeah, the one by the creek past the Campbell house?"

"Yes, there's a hole about head high that bees use to live in, remember?"

"Yeah."

"We can leave each other notes, like it's our post box. You check it each morning on your way to the McEwen's and I'll check it at night when I can. How's that sound?"

"Hunkey dorey!"

I stayed at Dead Goat Hollow for another day after Chester left. I packed up all my belongings in the feed bag, strapped my rifles to my back with Excalibur and said goodbye to my shelter.

I spent the next week roaming the forested hills on the south side of Franklin looking for the next place to camp. I stayed one night inside a hollow tree, a couple nights under a boulder that jutted out from the hill like an errant tooth. I eventually found a place to erect a small debris hut with cedar branches.

Every other night, I'd sneak to the Twisting Tree and

find it empty. I didn't leave Chester anything either, because I wasn't sure how long I'd be in one spot.

During the moon in its last stages of waning, I felt around inside the cavity. There was finally a note from Chester along with several pieces of blank paper and a cedar pencil. I stole away with the loot to my little hut on the hill.

In the light of my candle, his penmanship left something to be desired, but was legible enough.

Sorry it took so long, but that man was hard to find. I ventually did tho. His name is <u>Zeke Canfield</u>, if you want to know that. He has a bandage on his hand and on his nose, so he aint two hard to spot. Last I seen him was garding the Wilcox house on Church St. He seems to jist sit in a rockin chair on the porch all night drinking bug juice.

I felt a genuine smile spreading across my face. I turned the letter over where his words continued:

Like you asted, I told the entire McEwen house you was gone. It was the hardest thing I ever had to do. There was tears and wailing all about. <u>Addie bout had a come apart.</u>

Cammand me furtha.

Yur friend,

Chester Hamm

I SPENT THAT NIGHT UNDER A SLIVER OF MOON THAT LOOKED like a toenail clipping. I had made up my mind that I would start my one-man war at first light. I skipped breakfast and spent the morning scouting the town. From tree tops and rock outcroppings, I surveyed the town with the field glasses looking for the man with the birthmark. I didn't see him, but I did recognize a face on a construction detail in the Harpeth. It was one of the men who escorted Pa to the gallows. I remembered his large, hooked nose that made him look like a bird.

His crew was stacking stone on one side of the river that would presumably be used for a new bridge to Nashville. I crept to a bend in the river where the water had gouged dirt from the hillside, leaving a rock face about twenty feet above the water. I crawled up the side onto a ledge that was shielded by an overhanging sycamore branch.

I lay on the cold shelf of wet moss and propped myself on my elbows with the glasses to my eyes. I had a clear view of the construction site. The bird man was directing a few men moving large stones. I dislodged a stone the size of my head from the cliff wall and placed it in front of me. I laid the Whitworth's forestock on the rock. Unsatisfied with the stability, I peeled hunks of moss off the ledge and padded the top of the rock. The Whitworth then laid cradled in the moss, stable.

I sat up and looked around behind me, imagining my escape route. Where I would jump to, what logs I'd have to hop over or go under, which boulders to scale, which to go around. Once out of the river bank, I could take to the woods faster than any of those bluebellies could.

I watched the bird man for a minute through the field glasses to see if there was any routine in his movements. He was mostly standing in one spot ordering people around.

I took a deep breath. This was it, I thought. My mission of revenge would start in the upcoming minutes. Once it started, I couldn't go back. As if permitting me to carry out the deed, I heard my father's voice. *Don't let these Invaders—*

I tamped a load into the barrel of the Whitworth with the ramrod, cocked the hammer, and placed a cap on the nipple. I laid out shot and powder on a dry section of the ledge in case I could get off a second shot.

I lay prone and scooted up to the butt of the rifle. Right finger on the trigger guard, left hand on the forestock behind the rock. My cheek pressed against the stock, eyes finding the target. I lined up the sights on the bird man like I had done on many occasions with animals. The Whitworth felt steady as I readied for the shot.

I held the bird man in the sight picture, took a deep breath, and gently fingered the trigger. I slowly exhaled and squeezed the trigger, careful not to jerk. The blast of the gun kicked harder than I had anticipated. The rifle had kicked back off the rock and the rear site drove hard into my head just above my right eyebrow. The concussion was much louder among the rocks. My right ear seemed to burst inside.

I was in a daze as I watched the bird man collapse and fall into the water. His body submerged completely then bobbed back to the surface. The other men scrambled for the cover of the bank. Horrified faces scanned the surroundings for the source of the gunshot.

A small cloud of gun smoke lingered above me. They would use it to pinpoint my position. I was too shaken from the injuries I'd received from the recoil to attempt another shot. I gathered my stuff and jumped down from the ledge and followed the escape route until I was at the summit of a hill. I watched the river with the glasses to see if I was being followed.

Blue coats had swarmed the construction site. The bird man's body had been pulled from the river. Three or four were snooping around in the woods above the ledge I had shot from. After an hour, they still hadn't started up the hill in my direction. It afforded me time to calm down and consider my next move.

A stream of blood ran around and into my eye. I blotted it with my sleeve until there was just a clotted mat in my eyebrow. My ears still rang and I was a little dizzy. I laid my head on a mossy root to find my bearings. The gravity of what I had just done settled its weight on me. My chest was heavy, my lungs wanting to surrender. Each breath was a struggle. I tried to slow my breaths, increasing the depth of each one. I was exhausted from a storm of emotion. I could only stare upward.

The leaves above me had started turning yellow and orange. Smatterings of autumn colors punctuated the forest canopy. The cold temperatures would soon be upon me and the winter winds would blow through the naked forest. I needed to pull myself together and find better shelter.

Several hours into the night I was huddled in my debris hut when a single yelp pierced the quiet. Then another, closer to me. Another to the west. Like a fuse igniting explosives, the cries of the solitary coyotes picked up in volume and timbre and erupted into a symphony of howls and yipping. Their sinister song washed over the woodland. It was a coyote roll call. *Is everyone here?* They seemed to say. *Is everyone positioned to attack the little boy in the debris shelter? Tear his flesh from his bones and devour him?*

By and by, the coyote party subsided and the forest became still again. I got little sleep as I thought every noise in the forest was footsteps of approaching coyotes. Their heads inclined, bright eyes forward and focused. Lips pulled into a snarl. Streams of saliva flowing through sharp teeth. Or was it the bluebellies who had finally tracked me down, their rifles trained to shoot me between the eyes.

For fear of Invaders seeing the smoke, I had opted not to build a fire, making the dark woods and its inhabitants all the more threatening. Whether I slept that night or I dreamed of not sleeping, I didn't know. When the friendly sun finally poked over the horizon, assuring me I was safe, I slept for a while.

Around midday, feeling a little rested, I explored the hills searching for better shelter, picking up hickory nuts and persimmons along the way. My business with the Yankees was not yet over, so I didn't want to get too far from town.

In the late afternoon, I stumbled upon the perfect spot. A mile or so out, a merging of hills created a three-sided ravine. The back wall was a steep, limestone bluff. A spring flowed from under a stack of house-sized boulders near the rim, ran down through the center, and emptied into a larger creek beyond the opening of the hills.

The bluff was made up of a series of shelves on which thick cedar trees took root. Halfway up, there was a large crack in the rock face under an overhang. I made my way up and discovered it was more than a crack. It was a cave, its entrance just larger than my body.

I threw a few rocks inside to flush out any critters that might be hiding inside ready to attack. I found my candle, lit it and slowly advanced into the dark gap. The opening spread out inside, roughly the shape of a small bedroom. Its depth and width were several paces across. It was dry and musty. Possibly a former den for raccoons or foxes. It was perfect.

I sat just outside the opening for a few minutes to eat a persimmon and study the landscape. The ravine stretched several hundred yards into the forest toward the southeast, which meant I'd get the morning sun. It was also facing away from town, meaning a campfire's light would be concealed.

I made several trips to a stand of loblolly pines on a nearby ridge, filling the feed bag with needles. I made a pallet with them in the back of the cave and covered it with the quilt. Firewood was plentiful. A recent storm had toppled several oaks and hickories at the top of the ravine. Before sunset, I had built a small fire in the entrance of the cave under the shelter of the overhang.

When darkness fell, I walked a hundred yards down the ravine and looked back at my camp. A small orange glow was visible. After returning to the cave and moving the fire farther back into the chamber, I walked to several points in the forest to determine if the fire was visible. After dozens of attempts to get it just right, I had figured out the precise size and position in the cave I could have the fire without being seen from as little as thirty yards away.

I figured I'd hear someone coming at a hundred yards, but I didn't want to take any chances of being seen from outside of hearing range.

For the next few days, I gathered firewood and hickory nuts and stored them in the cave. I set up deadfall traps in four different spots within a half mile of my new home. I propped heavy rocks on flimsy sticks that balanced on a piece of bark. I placed the meat from a hickory nut on the bark so the weight of any rodent would upset the balance of the rock, flattening the quarry. I also set up two snares, that would have made Daniel Boone proud, on game trails hoping for an unsuspecting rabbit. Each morning I'd check the traps only to find them empty so I'd resort to boiling acorns or snails from the spring.

The ringing in my ears slowly faded away. My head had cleared and the gash on my forehead was a sticky scab. It was time to look for the man with the birthmark.

I roamed the hills, peering down on Franklin through gaps in the canopy where leaves had fallen away. The quiet town where I had gone to school, attended church, and played with friends, was now at the end of my rifle sites. Instead of familiar people milling about Main Street window shopping after church, through my field glasses there was nothing but the faces of strangers, enemies.

I spent an entire afternoon scanning the streets looking for the man with the birthmark. The sun low on the horizon, I gave up on him for the day and settled on a new sniper nest on a small rise overlooking the Charlotte Road where the Invaders had set up a small camp.

This time I propped the Whitworth in the elbow of a sapling to hold it steady and kneeled behind it. With it loaded and the hammer cocked, I used the field glasses to gauge my distance and choose a target. An officer had an audience of five soldiers gathered around, siting on logs and haunches, heads turned up at him. He wore a dirty white shirt and dark suspenders. He waved a cigar around as he talked to his men.

He was the better part of five hundred yards away. A distance I had never tried before, but wasn't afraid to attempt. "Queen Victoria hit her target from four hundred yards," I whispered to myself. I lined the sights up between his suspenders, then raised them just above his head to make up for the drop over distance.

I made sure my cheek was positioned farther back than last time. I slowed my breathing to a relaxed rhythm, covered the trigger with my finger, took a deep breath, slowly let it out, and squeezed the trigger.

The officer fell to the dirt before the sound of the Whitworth reached his cohorts. I tamped new powder and shot into the barrel and repeated the process. Invaders were frantically looking for the source of the shot. A bearded man pointed a finger in my direction, his jaw flapping up and down. I squeezed the trigger. Pointing at me was the last thing he did.

The camp was a scene of confusion and I was feeling confident. I prepared the rifle for another shot. A bee zipped past my ear. Then another one. The bark of a tree behind me splintered. They weren't bees, they were Minie balls. The Yankees were shooting at me.

I should have run, but I knew they would have a tough time pinpointing me. I took two deep breaths. On the second one, I let loose another round. A man's head jerked back, throwing off his hat. His limp body fell behind a wagon. Several men started running toward my position. I gathered up my things and flew through the forest, weaving through trees and jumping logs like hunted game. I ran full chisel for five minutes before I slowed to a walk. I had no fear of them gaining on me.

By the time I approached my cave, I was almost strolling. I was quite pleased with myself. Three more Yankees down. To cap off the day, a rabbit was flailing around in my snare. I was going to have a feast.

As I devoured the tender rabbit meat and drank wild mint tea, I calculated that day was my birthday. Under a cold, starry sky, on a ledge in the forest, I toasted myself. Happy thirteenth birthday, Vitus Swinggate.

What I didn't eat, I buried several yards from my lair so as not to attract critters. I set another log on the fire and lay on my pallet picking my teeth with a small bone. Orange fire light danced on the ceiling of the cave. I had indeed become my heroes, Mr. Boone and Mr. Crusoe. For the first time in recent memory, I slept dreamlessly with a full belly.

AT THE TWISTING TREE THE FOLLOWING NIGHT, I FOUND A leather saddlebag had been stuffed into the cavity. Inside, there was a candle, Lucifer matches, dried fruit, and bacon. Best of all, there was a leather-bound book, *Frankenstein; or Modern Prometheus* by Mary Shelley. Inside the cover was a note from Chester. There was enough moonlight to make most of it out.

Happy birthday pard. I thot you could use another book bout now. This is a good one on account of Haloween coming up and all. Addie keeps askin me bout you. Wether I'd heard anything from you or no. I keep tellin her no. Then she crys. And I keep telling her you are innocent and probly on a grate adventure. Then she says no your not. She says you are the sniper in the hills that is causing all the ruckus. Then she cries some more, saying you became a monster. I told her no you wernt.

You need to skeedaddle. Everyone knows it's you up on the hills shootin people. Some folks are calling you the fiend in the forest. The grapevine says they's organizen a big manhunt for you. I hope you git out of town to safety.

Yur frend, Chester Hamm

I DIDN'T WRITE HIM BACK. I MULLED OVER THE IDEA OF BEING a demon. It saddened me that I had been ostracized from the people I grew up with. And it was especially upsetting that Addie was scared of me. But as I ruminated, anger churned and mixed with grief, gaining momentum until sorrow turned to a molten rage. I had the right to feel the way I did and act how I did. I was defending my honor. My family. Now the town of Franklin had turned against me. I'd give them something to talk about. Something to fear.

For three days, I stayed away from my lair on an Invader hunting spree. From a small hillock, I picked off a man on a horse who was riding up the Columbia Pike. From the cemetery, I shot a sentry walking along Bridge Street. Perched on the roof of an abandoned slave cabin, I made my most challenging shot on a sentry on the ramparts of Fort Granger.

Unfortunately, none of the men were the one with the

birthmark and the Fort Granger shot was the last bullet I had for the Whitworth. I slid my trusty rifle into a crack inside the cave for safekeeping. The rifle I had picked up from the Yankee soldier on the road did not have the range of the Whitworth and there were only a handful of Minie balls left. I conceded that my sniper days were over for now.

I lay on my pallet listening to the crackle of the fire and opened *Frankenstein*. I read for hours before I fell asleep with it on my chest. The next morning was cold. The fire had burned itself completely out. I used a match to light a pine cone that would serve as kindling. I piled more logs on until the warmth enveloped me. With a cup of pine needle tea, I read more *Frankenstein*, breathing white puffs of mist.

SHELLEY'S WORDS RESONATED WITH ME. FRANKENSTEIN'S monster, through no fault of his own, was an outcast and a killer. He was created by circumstances outside his control. Like me, he was forced into hiding, wandering the forest, watching villagers, and taking their lives. Many times, he was referred to as a fiend. There was that word again—fiend. I hadn't really understood what it meant when Chester said the people of Franklin called me the Fiend of the Forest. Mary Shelley spelled it out for me. I understood it now. I owned it.

. . .

Counting days from my birthday, Halloween was two nights away. What a perfect way to introduce the Fiend of the Forest to the people of Franklin.

In the dark sky of All Hallow's Eve, thick groups of clouds swept overhead. White cotton balls turning dark gray as they passed under a bright half-moon.

I dug to the bottom of the feed bag, where I had stuffed Ma's black funeral cloak. I threw it over my shoulders, tied it at the front and pulled the hood down to my eyes. It was a little big, but it concealed me from head to knees. I used charcoal from my fire pit to color my face black, only my eyes visible. I cut a strip from the bottom of the cloak and tied it around my face covering nose to chin. I strapped Excalibur to my back, and the hunting knife at my waist. I was ready to descend upon the sleepy little village.

Handwritten notes at top:
- he was trying to find birthmark guy
- he kills another Yankee
- he finds birthmark guy and kills him
- he is now hurt his ankle + in the woods, but he is feeling lonley + depressed after his actions.
- he says "but something about it felt unfinished."

TWENTY-TWO

Yankees by campfires didn't notice the dark phantom glide past them in the field. A sentry never heard my feet on the cobbles as I rushed up behind him and then darted left into an alley. The Morgan family gathered together in their kitchen, never suspected the presence of a specter observing them from the shadowy limbs of a tree.

I moved through the streets in search of my quarry, pausing at intersections to wait for a cloud to cover the moon before I crossed. Yankees were gathered in front of the Hiram Masonic Lodge, smoking and drinking around a fire they had built on the front steps. Laughing and telling ghost stories, unaware I was watching, scanning their faces for a birthmark.

Avoiding street lamps, I moved down Church Street and crept to the porch of the Wilcox house. Though my expectations were low, I was still disappointed to see the rocking chair empty.

Handwritten side note: he's still trying to find birthmark guy

A voice cried out from my left. "You, there! Halt!" I ran between houses looking for an escape route. Boots clomped on the cobble stones behind me as I shot down an alley.

Another patrolling party was heading toward me from another direction. I painted myself to a wall under a low, overhanging roof and became invisible in the inky black shadow. The Yankee pursuing me slowed and stopped in the alley a few paces in front of my position, white puffs of breath pumping out of him like a steam engine. The party had moved on up the street.

He looked right at me, or what he thought was me. I held my breath. His face contorted in confusion. He must have seen me throw myself into the dark space, but somehow couldn't distinguish my form from the shadow.

He swung his rifle off his shoulder, aimed it in my direction and stepped closer to investigate, bewilderment on his face. I closed my eyes for fear they'd reflect the street lamps. My heart pounded, the rest of me paralyzed. The voices from the patrol party faded.

His boots clicked on the stones within reach of me. I opened my eyes. In the dim light, his eyes grew to huge orbs. The barrel of his rifle was at chest level, an arm's length away. I stepped into the pale light, revealing myself. His face recoiled in horror at the sight of the phantom before him. A demon clad in black from head to foot with no visible face, only eyes. To him, I was the grim reaper, and his time had come this Halloween night.

In one fluid motion, I redirected his rifle and grabbed his throat with the other hand and squeezed. I felt my thumb and index finger connect behind his trachea. He dropped the rifle, the butt landing hard on my foot. I drove him backward as he clawed at my hands and face, trying to relieve the pressure.

I grabbed his arm with my free hand and stepped my foot behind his, tripping him. I drove him to the ground, my hand still clutched around his windpipe. His head hit with a thud. I sat on his chest and applied pressure to his throat with both hands. He bucked and thrashed, pulling uselessly at my wrists. His eyes bulged, red veins visible in the lamplight. Then he stopped.

I dragged his body out of sight and left him in an alcove then made my way out of the alley. Keeping to narrow passages between buildings, I proceeded to the McEwen house. From behind the boxwoods, I watched the house. Shutters were pulled tightly against the windows. A fiery pang of lonesomeness filled my gut. The only people left in the world that I cared about were safe inside, shielded from the bitter cold. Fortified from the evils of the world. From fiends and outcasts like me.

For several hours, I walked with the other ghosts that surely haunted the town, moving through shadowed corridors and dark recesses looking for the man with the birthmark.

A faint, orange glow in the east was barely discernible when dumb luck—maybe destiny—brought me upon a man with familiar features.

I was scanning Main Street from the roof of a building near West Margin when I noticed a man sitting on the front steps of the Presbyterian Church across the street. He was slumped as if asleep, his forage cap pulled down over his forehead. The collar of his coat was flipped up to his ears.

[margin note: he killed another Penn.]

In one hand, a cigarette was nearly burned to his fingers. The other hand was tucked inside his sleeve.

I studied him for a minute. A miserable wretch. A bluebelly piece of scum using the steps of a church in my town as a bed. As a toilet. Zeke Canfield, Chester had said his name was.

I climbed down to the back alley, ran around the block of buildings. I stayed against the storefronts on a quiet Main Street and worked my way toward the church. Dim lamp light stretched into the display window of Whitton's General Store. The chess pieces hadn't changed since I had made my last maneuver so many moons ago. I crossed the street and stayed close to the brick walls.

Between the last shop in the row and the Presbyterian Church there was a walkway leading to the back of the buildings. I slid along the wall until I was directly to his right side about five paces away. He was sawing logs.

I didn't want to attack him in the open, so I devised a plan to lure him into the alcove between the structures. I continued sliding along the wall into the passageway, beyond the light of the lamps.

The corridor was just wider than my arm span. I placed one foot on the brick face of the wall, made a little hop and stuck my other foot to the opposite wall, suspending myself above the walkway. Slowly and laboriously, I shimmied a dozen feet or more toward the rooftops.

I called out in a whispered yell, "Canfield. Canfield." I listened for movement. I could make out a little shuffling and scraping. "Canfield, come here. I need your help."

He stumbled into view and wobbled drunkenly out of the lamp light down the corridor. I clung to the walls with my feet, legs spread wide and aching. Closer and closer, he approached. I couldn't see his face, but was confident he never saw the hooded assassin suspended between the walls above him.

I slowly drew Excalibur from my back, took in a deep breath and pulled my feet off the walls. I dropped into the darkness below me. For a flash, I could make out lines and contours of his form as I rapidly plummeted toward him. The edge of Excalibur drove into his head, his forage cap dulling the cracking sound. The sword gave a little in my hands. I landed on my feet harder than I had anticipated and toppled backward. He staggered and fell into a pile of trash.

Getting to my feet, I realized the fall had done something to my ankle. In that heightened state, I felt no pain, but the ankle refused to hold my weight, turning flaccidly inward with each step I took toward Canfield's body. A dim ribbon of lamplight ran the length of his back. I could discern subtle movements.

I grabbed his shoulder and turned him over, his birthmark standing out in the pale light. It was more disgusting than I had thought. It wasn't as much the shape of a tick as I remembered it. It was more like a stretched-out garden spider. This close up, it didn't seem as large either.

His eyes were wide with fear, glistening and twitching. He was in shock. The blow to his head had crippled his capacity for function.

Incoherent mumbling passed through his chapped lips, and a narrow stream of blood ran from under his hat into the corner of one eye. His nose, healed from our previous encounter, bore a hairy mole on the tip. Snot and blood ran from his nostrils.

I pulled the hood off my head and slid the cover off my face.

"Do you recognize me, Zeke?" I said in the most serious, grown-up voice. His eyes bulged, and his head shook. He tried to scoot away from me only to meet resistance from a pile of refuse. He opened his mouth to scream, but failed to get the words out. I jammed the pointed end of Excalibur into his mouth.

His hands wrapped around the wooden blade and pulled at it. His grip was strong. Both wrists were sturdy against my pull, and oddly enough, neither had a bandage on it. I stepped on one arm and held the sword firmly in his mouth. He gagged and choked on the splintery, red oak shaft. He thrashed and kicked. The bottom of his boot caught my left shin, peeling the skin off under my trousers. I pressed the sword harder.

His right hand slid down his side and pulled back his coat revealing a revolver. I drew Excalibur and raised it over my head. Just before he pulled the pistol out, I brought the blade down hard.

The impact did not feel as solid as I would have expected. His body twitched and convulsed, the trash underneath clinking and rustling. I hit him a third time directly on the birthmark. Excalibur's blade gave again. I realized the blade was cracked. It was nearly in two, but it had finished the job.

A dark gash ran diagonally across the ugly birthmark. He no longer moved. I looked down on him, between white puffs of my breath. No mist passed through his lips or nose. Like the rest of the garbage he lay among, his body was lifeless and would soon rot and pollute the air with his foul stench.

I hobbled through the streets toward the forest, empowered with a temporary feeling of relief and joy from dispatching the man with the birthmark. With the chemicals in my body returning to normal levels and my excitement waning, the pain in my ankle became excruciating. I could barely put any weight on it. By the time I had reached the field separating the town from the hills, I was hopping on one foot. I was eventually forced to crawl, my knees sinking into the soft dirt.

In the forest I peeled two pieces of thick bark from a shagbark hickory and tied them on each side of my ankle with the sash I had been wearing on my face. I found a hefty branch I could use as a walking stick, and slowly picked my way through the wooded hills, connecting the dots of moonlight that trickled through the dark lattice of branches.

In the safety of my lair, I collapsed on my pallet, carefully removed my boot, and propped my foot on a stone. Gauging by touch, the ankle seemed twice the normal size, puffy and soft. Throbbing came in waves.

I slowed my breathing and tried to wind down for sleep. When I closed my eyes, encore after encore of the night's events played out in my head. The man with the birthmark's ruined face repeatedly flashed and the cracking sound of bones reverberated in my skull. He was still very much alive in my dreams.

I had to open my eyes to interrupt the horror show. The crescent-shaped opening of the cave was like a portal into another world, luminescent in contrast to my dark chamber. Outside, twisted and gnarled limbs crowded the foreground, and stars twinkled in the background. Silver moonlight piled on naked branches like snow. The solace I was supposed to have earned from killing the man with the birthmark had thus far evaded me. I had never felt so lonely as I did lying in that dank cave, like Frankenstein's monster.

The beautiful peephole into a more peaceful world blurred and eventually faded. I fell into a fitful sleep full of nightmares, only to wake in the gloomy morning feeling the heavy weight of loneliness and depression. Something about my act of revenge was unsettling to me. It wasn't the heinousness of the crime alone, but something about it felt unfinished.

TWENTY-THREE

The next couple of weeks passed with monotonous routine as my ankle healed. I struggled with sleeplessness at night on account of reoccurring nightmares involving the violent deaths in my life. In the mornings, I hobbled to the traps to see if I'd eat that day or not.

An imaginary Addie and Chester often accompanied me in my tasks. I'd ask their opinions, complain to them, and celebrate with them. Sometimes the illusion of Chester wasn't there and I could have some alone time with pretend Addie. I talked to her as if we were a couple and shared more intimate details of my thoughts. I'd even catch myself showing off for her, trying to impress her with my resourcefulness or how tough I was.

As I became more mobile, I prepared for the harsh winter to come. I stockpiled firewood, cramming logs into every nook and cranny of the cave. I built a wall in front of the entrance with branches I had laboriously removed from the nearby cedar trees. I lined the floors and walls of my cavern with more pine and cedar branches.

I moved the stones of my fire pit farther inside the cave where even a small fire could fill the chamber with heat, but close enough to the exit for the smoke to filter through the cedar branches.

"That'll keep us plenty warm," I'd say to my make-believe friends. "The lair is complete."

If I wasn't crawling and limping around for firewood, I spent much of the daylight hours lying by the fire reading and rereading my books. I'd sometimes play parlor games with my imaginary friends.

We played Grandmother's Trunk. Naturally, I began with the first item. "My grandmother keeps an apple in her trunk." Then imaginary Addie, would say "My grandmother keeps an apple and a bible in her trunk." Pretend Chester's turn: "My grandmother keeps an apple, a bible, and collard greens in her trunk." On and on it would continue up the alphabet until I'd get bored.

With branches from an Osage orange tree and a poplar, I spent countless hours carving small chess pieces, starting with the king and queen and finishing with pawns. One army was poplar, while the other was Osage orange. I scratched out a playing board on a flat slab of slate. When the entire set was finished, I started an imaginary game with the Colonel.

An Indian summer day ended with the approach of a menacing storm. Lightning soon lit the sky, slithering through the clouds like snakes, then reaching to the ground. For an instant the strings of electricity hung in the air. The image of yellow tree roots burned into my eyes.

With every strike the forest illuminated, casting sinister shadows of creeping monsters on its floor, filling the lair with hot white. The thunder was impossibly loud. It came in short intervals, blasting a rifle-loud cacophony through my home, shaking the walls.

The rain fell heavily in torrents. Water cascaded over the front doorway. The wind howled past the opening of the lair, carrying branches and debris. Northerly gusts blew water deep inside. Despite my careful placement of the fire, it was soon extinguished.

I lit a candle to see that water intruded my living space from the back walls. Rivulets ran down the rock and formed a stream on the floor. I lifted my pallet before it was entirely wet, and scooted farther back and up into the cave.

For hours, the malicious storm raged on. Just as I was growing weary and had thoughts of attempting sleep, there came a new sound. At first it was the rumble of thunder, but it grew in intensity and became constant. I could best describe it as an oncoming train. I suddenly felt like I was under a railroad track bridge and the train was crossing above me.

The pressure inside the lair changed to the extent I thought my ears would burst and I'd be sucked out by the claws of the tempest. I was enveloped by a roar so loud I thought I'd have brain damage. The cave walls seemed to shake violently. My candle blew out. I curled into a fetal position against the back wall under the pallet. The storm raged and shook the very earth inside of which I sought refuge. God's hand seemed to reach through the dark skies and would soon pluck me from my lair for all the sins I had committed and deliver me to the demons of hell.

I had all but given up on the idea of communicating with God since my family was ripped from me, but huddled in the dark hole, I heard myself softly pleading. Unconsciously, words escaped my lips, asking that I be forgiven for my offenses and be spared of this storm. The winds raged more furiously. Leaves, pine needles, and dirt swirled around inside the cave in a ferocious eddy. God had passed his judgement. I was doomed.

"Ma, Pa, James," I said, my voice consumed by the roar. "Please protect me!"

The howling train passed after several minutes. As it bellowed toward the north, I fell into contemplation about God and his existence. Had He spared me? Had He even listened? Did He exist? If He did, why kill my family? Why this war?

Instead of God, was my family watching over me from above as my archangels? Or had I spared myself by providing cover in which to hunker against the menacing weather? Or was it something else I don't yet understand? Something came to mind that Robinson Crusoe had said after he was spared from a grave ague. He too, questioned the works of God until he found a passage in the bible. *Lord look upon me, Lord pity me, Lord have mercy upon me.* If I put some effort into retrieving the memory, I'm sure I could come up with a similar message relayed by our reverend at St. Paul's or by Abe. But as it was, I wasn't yet ready to acknowledge the existence of God and His involvement in the weather and the fate of my soul.

The madness of the storm eventually abated, leaving me exhausted from the tension. I inclined my head toward the heavens and let out a quiet *Thank you* without designation of whom I was thanking. Perhaps my parents and my brother.

The clear morning found me picking through arboreal debris, exploring the forest. Dozens of trees throughout the ravine had fallen. Some caught in the arms of other canopies. Some broken in half. At the top of the hill above my lair, a large, discernible path of downed trees had been carved through the woods. A great swath, the width of sixty yards or so, had been cut along the ridge, beginning out of sight to the south and disappearing over the rise to the north. It was quite evident a cyclone of significant magnitude had landed hard upon the earth and chewed its way through the forest, spitting flora and fauna every which way.

A shiver ran through me as a cold breeze picked up and swirled among the vast supply of firewood the cyclone had left me.

THE CYCLONE HAD TAUGHT ME THAT I WASN'T QUITE prepared for the winter months to come. In order to survive, I had to make some adjustments to the lair.

As the sun set on a brisk day, I travelled toward town on frosty paths dressed in my dark clothes. I crept around a large Union camp just outside of town. In a supply tent, I found a pickaxe and small shovel, and in an officer's tent, a chamber pot and wool blanket. I was in no mood to press my luck, so I wasted no time in leaving.

Back at the cave, I went straight to work. First, I dug out a small bed chamber atop a rock shelf to raise my sleeping quarters off the floor. Beneath it, I dug a small pit for two purposes: to allow a well for cold air to sink into, and in combination with small trenches I carved out, to redirect intruding water.

The trenches all led to a chamber in the cave that drained into the earth somewhere. I later discovered where when I went to drink from the stream outside and noticed a brown runnel of water trickling from under a bush. After a little investigation, I realized the drain inside the lair connected to the stream.

I carried dirt with the chamber pot and piled it in front of the entrance, closing it up, until only a small aperture remained at the top. I fastened a door of cedar branches and moss. On the inside of the mound I now had to climb to enter or exit the lair, I carved a hearth and stacked stone to fashion a makeshift fireplace. With a few adjustments, I was able to make small fires with long-dried wood and most of the smoke would make its way outside.

I cleared off several more rock shelves and stuffed them full of firewood. I piled green and wet wood left by the storm on a large shelf near the hearth to dry. Deadfall wood that had already seasoned was split and stacked thickly on the other shelves. In the area I called my kitchen, I had a basket full of walnuts and acorns I had collected, a few strips of venison hanging from a rope, and two canteens full of spring water.

For a couple nights, I'd lay in my new bed and watch the fire burn itself out, but a thought nagged and nagged. With the entrance so small, and above my line of sight from the bed, I felt insecure about the prospect of someone finding the hole before I detected their approach, thus trapping me inside.

With a good deal of labor, I worked to widen the drain in the back of the cave until I could squeeze through it to the outside. It was a little rough and wet, and was the length of a dozen yards, but it would serve as an emergency escape hatch if someone infiltrated the front entrance.

Climbing in through the escape hatch would be difficult for anyone. It would be difficult to find, require a skinny build, and was slippery. It was doubtful anyone could infiltrate the passage without making quite a bit of noise.

It wasn't long before I realized the hatch *could* be penetrated. I was lying in bed reading when a skinny raccoon with a disheveled pelage ambled through my parlor, as I called it, and up the side of a wall into a hole no wider than my head. He did this without even a sideways glance at me. As if he owned the place and was put out by my presence.

In the following weeks, he came and went as he pleased. Sometimes, he'd stop and look at me, look around my parlor and kitchen with his big, glassy eyes, then carry on about his business without a care in the world. He always seemed sedated and confused, like the town drunk. His overall demeanor was that of an old man. And for that I named him Grandpa.

For the most part, Grandpa kept to himself in his little apartment. Every once in a while, he'd sit in his hole and watch me. Other times, he'd wake me in the middle of the night invading my stores. I'd throw something at him, like a cup or pebble. In response, he'd stop, glance over his shoulder, and give me a look that I could only describe as one a grandpa would give that says, *do that again, and I'll take you over my knee, boy.* He was an ill-tempered little fella, but it was nice having a roommate.

WINTER CAME, AND WITH IT SNOW AND BALEFUL WINDS. I had become a hibernating bear, nay raccoon, nestled in my den, only coming out occasionally to search the barren landscape for food. The forest was a different world in the winter. It was often completely silent. No chirping, no insects buzzing. Just silence sometimes broken by whispers in the tree tops from the breeze. On some windless days, listening to the forest was like the soundlessness you get when you dunk your head underwater. It was a stillness so complete that leaves thawing and expanding under the warmth of the morning sun crackled loudly in contrast.

While walking aimlessly one afternoon, the trickling of a small spring in a cliff drew me to its delicious supply. Among the nearby ferns, I found a cedar branch that was about six feet long, had a few twigs on it, and was unusually straight with little tapering. I shucked the twigs and remaining bark off with a flat piece of slate rendering it smooth and comfortable to hold. I immediately employed it as my walking staff. Traversing the forest became much easier and took some stress off my ankle allowed it to heal faster.

Even after my ankle had fully recovered, I used my staff as I roamed. I'd sometimes hold it in both hands and strike shrubs and vines with its ends. With practice I was soon spinning it in figure eight motions or like a wheel in front and in back of me. My staff had become a fighting tool.

Staff in hand, I leisurely strolled along a hunting path about half a mile from the lair. I usually traveled quietly and on guard, but I was quite startled when three bedding deer burst from the forest floor no less than thirty yards from me. As their big white tails flashed through the tree trunks down the side of the hill, I realized the importance of silence. I was down wind of the deer, yet they became aware of my presence too early. Had I been hunting, I would have ruined my chances. What if, instead of deer hiding in the brush, it was Canfield's cronies in the form of a Yankee foraging party? I had to become more like the forest animals if I wanted to survive. Especially in the eerie silence of a winter wood.

The lack of noise during the time of year was a double edged sword. It was an advantage that I could hear anything that moved, but when you're prey, everything sounds like a predator. A chipmunk's burp could sound like a grown man coughing. A squirrel skipping across the leaf litter sounded like a horse. Passing deer conjured images of elephants.

Soon enough, I could recognize the volume and cadence of noise created by neighboring critters. The predictable rhythm and amplitude of human footfalls, were they to approach, would clearly differ from wildlife.

On the other hand, the stillness of the forest made me

feel vulnerable when out and about. It was for this reason that I learned to move among the trees like a ghost.

I created paths radiating in several directions from the lair like the spokes of a wagon wheel. Each contained a certain pattern of movement. I'd jump from rock to rock, root to root, rock to root, pad along a patch of moss, or run atop a fallen tree or boulder. In some places, I used my staff to pole vault from place to place.

After much practice, I could move a hundred yards from the lair noiselessly and as fast as a deer. If there was no moss or rock to quiet my steps, I'd clear patches of leaves so that I could walk on pads of soil. I traveled like this until I reached the well-worn game trails that had already been established.

My unique form of locomotion had another benefit—no foot prints. It was easy for me to track animals, and a boot print would clearly stand out to a hunter. I took great care to never leave a visible foot print. Rarely did I walk in the middle of a trail. If I was forced to create an impression of my boot, I'd painstakingly brush it away.

One night, an early ice storm covered the ground with a surface I could walk on with no fear of leaving tracks. It was a good night to roam to town. Finding nothing in the Twisting Tree, I came across a Union camp on the opposite side of a pond. Luckily I saw the smoke of their fire, before they could hear me.

Hoping to avoid the crunching of the forest underfoot, I checked the strength of the ice on the pond. I pressed on it with my staff. When it seemed solid, I stepped onto the slippery surface. It held my weight. Carefully, I eased my way across—the moon reflecting off the ice like a sheet of glass. The camp was quiet. Everyone was asleep.

The area around their tents was well trod upon which made it quieter to walk on. The fire had almost died out, but was enough to warm my hands for a moment. I sat on my haunches, enjoying the relief from the cold. For a fleeting moment, I reveled in the fantasy that I was a part of the camp. That I too had just finished a night of eating and chatting with my pals around a fire before retiring to a mattress inside my warm tent.

I shook the dream off and surveyed the area. There were eight tents, shaped like little A-frame houses. The two biggest ones had stove pipes poking through the roof. A table and two chairs sat in front of the tent closest to me. A gas lamp, a couple of plates, cups and spoons sat on the table top. A basket hung from the back of a chair.

Inside were three goose eggs and some hard tack. I gently placed a plate, cup, and spoon in the basket and lifted it from the chair. I crept back to the pond where I drifted back across to the shelter of the dark woods.

TWENTY-FOUR

During the daylight hours, I kept myself as busy as possible with hunting, gathering wood, practicing my staff fighting, and redecorating the lair. All in an attempt to stave off the crushing loneliness. The only challenge greater than dealing with hunger, was grappling with the smothering isolation. I was having a harder time dealing with it than Robinson Crusoe had on his desolate island.

As winter dragged on, I longed more and more for the company of real people. Some days I'd start toward town. Along the way, heated discussions with illusory Chester and Addie ensued. Ultimately, we'd talk me out of the expedition, convincing me I was indeed the Fiend of the Forest, Mary Shelly's monster that had no place in society. I had earned my station in life. I was a murderer who deserved solitary confinement.

In the middle of the second moon cycle since Halloween, a storm dumped snow for two days straight.

The forest was blanketed with white powder as deep as my knee. Food was nearly impossible to find. When my walnuts and acorns ran out, I survived four days on a mouse and a salamander I had trapped in the cave. On the fifth day, I threw the last piece of firewood on the coals.

The snow lingered for many days. Scavenging for food and wood was no longer an option. Cold to the marrow and starved, I was forced to make my way to town. I hid my rifles and broken Excalibur inside a crevice in the back of the cavern. I tucked my knife and pistol in my waist, a candle and matches in my pocket, staff in my hand. I wrapped myself in my cloak and quilt and left the cave. As the sun set, I traveled through the frigid woods, timing my arrival at dark.

I found the Twisting Tree. Inside the cavity, a bulging hemp sack occupied most of the space. It required reshaping to extract it. I slung it over my shoulder and headed to one of our old fishing spots on the Harpeth. I crawled into the space under the sprawling roots of the sycamore on the bank. Under candlelight, I removed the contents of the bag.

Along with several letters, there was a haversack containing a potato, salted pork, ginger bread, and hard tack. I immediately started tearing at the pork and hard tack. "Thank you, Chester," I said under my breath, my words sounding muffled in the small space among the roots and rocks. All of the food had varying amounts of fuzzy mold on the surface. I scraped the bulk of it off with my knife.

After several bites, I was able to turn my focus toward the letters. They had gotten wet and stained. Between soiling and Chester's bad penmanship, it took effort to interpret their messages.

V,

    Meet me at Campbell pond tomorro nite. It is very important. Yur in a heap of trouble.

    Yur frend, Chester

I UNFOLDED ANOTHER LETTER:

V,

What have you gottin yurself into? Was it you? If so, I gess you kno what Im talking about. The wole town of Franklin is in a frinzy about the killings. Im leaving you sum clipings from the town paper. I hope yur ok and yur not going to do no more of it. I wish youd tell me whare you are so we can talk.

    Yur frend,
    Chester

THE CLIPPINGS WERE FROM THE SMALL NEWSPAPER THE Yankees distributed throughout Franklin once a week. It was usually a bunch of propaganda and stories meant to sway the locals toward the Union political cause.

The first clipping was torn and smudged. The headline read, "SNIPER KILLS 7 FEDERAL SOLDIERS!" The article listed the victim's names, the military units they had belonged to, and the locations where they were shot. The reporter claimed the sniping was carried out by the "Fiend of the Forest" and that there was a substantial reward for information regarding my whereabouts. It then reminded everyone how the streets were safer because of the presence of the fine Union Army.

"MURDER IN THE STREETS OF FRANKLIN" the next article said. "…a cold-blooded killer walks among us…" This one made me out to be a monster that lurked in the shadows waiting to kill any innocent citizen. It failed to point out that it was only uniformed Yankees that I had dispatched. Again, the report painted the picture that the grand United States Army was here to protect the people of Franklin.

I threw the article down and held another letter closer to the candle.

Happy Thanksgiving pard. Heres some pork and a potato for you. I hope you git it.

Yur frend,
Chester

I STUFFED MORE FOOD IN MY MOUTH. I UNFOLDED THE NEXT letter. The handwriting was different. It was neat and well ordered. Girly even. I skipped to the end to see who it was from. In curly letters it read, "Yours Truly, Adelicia McEwen."

My heart galloped. Despite the cold, my palms sweated. I scanned back to the top.

Dear Vitus,

I hope this letter finds you well. I am quite concerned for your safety. I understand the circumstances in which you have found yourself and I am sorry the recent tragedies have befallen you. I am also well aware of your devious actions and hope that you are repentant for them. I neither understand nor condone such unscrupulous deeds, but maybe you will find your way back to God. When you do, I would like to see you again. Unfortunately you are no longer welcome at our home, or the town of Franklin for that matter. It would please me to someday ride Thoreau with you in the fields beyond town. I will pray for you and your soul.

Yours Truly,
Adelicia McEwen

I VOMITED ON THE ROCKS BESIDE THE WATER, CAREFUL NOT TO get any on Addie's letter. Either I couldn't handle the excitement her letter caused, or it had been too long since I had had a proper meal. Regardless, my stomach couldn't handle it.

I was a little confused by her letter. Did this mean she still cared for me and really wanted to be with me, or was it only an act of charity? And why was she privy to my and Chester's secret correspondence? She shouldn't even know we were communicating.

I tore off another piece of pork and chewed on it while I read the last letter. Chester again.

Merry Christmas pard! I hope you like the ginger bred and tack I lef. I've been coming here nearly every day to see if you come or not. I gess not today neether. I will leav you anuther leter and gift on new years. I will be staying at home betwixt chrismas and new years eve. I hope you aint froz yur rear off!

Yur friend,
Chester

. . .

TEARS WELLED IN MY EYELIDS. MY FRIEND, HAD MADE THE trek to the Twisting Tree in a snow storm to deliver me a Christmas care package. I badly wanted to be with him and the rest of the kids from the McEwen house (except for McKlusky—he could kiss my boot) gathered around a warm fireplace singing carols. Even more, I wanted to be with my family during the holidays. But, like Christmas, my family was gone. I had spent Christmas alone, starving and cold in a cave.

There were no more letters, so I figured it wasn't January yet and that Chester was home. I chewed on another piece of pork, careful to swallow only a scant amount at a time to placate my sensitive stomach. I needed to see Chester.

Invigorated with a plan, I gathered my stuff and left my hideout. I crossed the field, found the road to be empty, and started running west. I didn't slow until the gray outline of Chester's house was before me. I stood in the shadows until I could catch my breath. Mist spewed from me in clouds. The cold air was like needles in my lungs.

I stood outside Chester's window, my stomach in knots. I hadn't seen another human in weeks, Chester in months. Would he even recognize me? My hair had grown long. If I was older, I'd have a beard. Instead, my face was coated with grime. I pulled the hood off my head and tapped lightly on his window.

It took a few seconds, but a familiar form appeared on the other side of the glass. Instead of the smile I had expected, there was a look of horror and surprise on his face. He must have thought he was looking at a ghost. Maybe he had come to accept that his best friend was a monster. A killer who lurked in the woods. Whatever was going through his mind, he froze in petrification. I was suddenly filled with shame. He saw me as a heartless, feral animal. I almost turned and ran away. I took a deep breath and gave him a wave and a smile as I stepped closer to the window. "It's me," I whispered. "It's Vitus."

Slowly his face softened and his lips turned upward. He held up a finger, "jus a sec," he mouthed. He disappeared into the darkness of his house. A moment later he was back. He waved his hand, indicating I come in. When he saw the question on my face, he waved faster.

I walked around the corner of the house to the door. It slowly moved inward revealing a sliver of black within. Chester filled the gap with his big head, then pulled the door wider. I softly stepped inside.

"He's passed out. Come on," he whispered, referring to his pa. We snuck to his room where he lit a lantern and closed the door. We shook hands and sat on his bed. The ropes that supported his mattress had not been tightened in a long time. We sunk nearly to the floor, the cords complaining with a loud creak.

He had become very excited and wanted to know all the details of the last few months. We sat and talked a while. At one point, his pa moved around in the other room. We waited for him to go silent again before we resumed our conversation. He listened to my tales with wide eyes and toothy grins. I hated to change the subject, but I had important matters to discuss.

"What's everybody sayin' bout me?" I asked.

"They're after you."

"Who?"

"Everybody. The big storm slowed everything down a bit, but they aim to start the search back up after the new year. You gotta get out of town, Vit."

"I've got an idea."

"Shoot."

"Do you know if they ever found the bodies of those men I killed on the road by my house?"

"No. In fact I know for sure. I heard the Colonel talking to some bluebellies 'bout it. Says they never fount 'em. Why ya ask?"

"I'm going to die."

"Come again, pard?"

"We're gonna make the whole town believe I'm dead."

"How do you plan to go 'bout that?"

"You have any extra clothes around?" I asked as I scanned his room.

"Just that ratty old pair of trousers that don't fit me no more and that shirt I wear to church." He pointed to a lump of material in the corner. I held them up.

"These will work well enough," I said. "Can I borrow 'em?"

"Sure. Well enough for what, Vit?"

"You'll see. Can you do me a favor?"

"Sure, pard."

"It's not going to be easy."

"What is it?"

"Tell everyone that you was out lookin' for me and found my body."

His face contorted with concern.

"Listen," I said. "If everyone thinks I'm dead, maybe they'll call off the manhunt."

He smiled and bobbed his head up and down.

"Just say you found my body in Dead Goat Hollow and that I was so rotten that you had to leave me there."

"That makes sense, I guess. How did you die?"

"Umm… let's tell em Zeke Canfield killed me."

"But he's dead ain't he?" Chester's eyes widened.

"He could have done it before I killed him."

"But that would mean you didn't kill him and someone else did."

I'm not sure if his train of thought was going where mine went, but he had made one of the smartest observations he'd ever made.

"You're right," I said, giving him credit. "If someone else killed him, they'd keep up the manhunt for whoever did it and they might end up finding me anyway."

We sat in silence for a moment mulling it over.

I broke the silence. "It's okay. I'm guilty of all my sins and I have to own up to it. It's better that they know I did all the killin' so they won't look for no one anymore. I have to be the killer, and I have to be dead."

"You could kill yerself. Hunting accident? Starve to death?"

"Just don't tell them anything 'bout how I died. After all, you ain't a detective. Let 'em figure it out on their own."

"That makes sense."

"What day is it, anyway?" I asked him.

"Umm…I think tomorrow is New Year's Eve."

"Okay, can you wait 'till New Year's day to tell them? Just keep out of sight tomorrow, then go into town and tell the Colonel you found me."

"Okay."

"Even Addie, Chester. You have to promise, as hard as it might be for her to hear it. You have to tell her and her family I'm dead."

He let out a gasp, then returned his attention. He nodded.

"Honor bright?" I said. "You'll do it?"

"Honest injun, Vit. I'll do you proud."

"It's gonna be mighty difficult, you know? You're gonna have to do some fine acting. Everybody is gonna be crying and carryin' on."

"I know."

"You'll have to cry too." I gave him a playful shove and smiled. "Be a big blubberin' mess on account of your life being so empty without your ole pard." We both chuckled a little. "You'll have to organize a grand funeral for me. Have an awe-inspiring ceremony to celebrate my life." We erupted in laughter. "Don't forget the monument."

There was a thump in the other room. We froze, looking at each other, trying to contain our laughs. A wave of humiliation poured over me. Suddenly, I couldn't look him in the eye. The cold, hard truth was that no one was going to cry over my death. There'd be no funeral. No fuss.

The laughter felt good, though. Gallows humor, I supposed. We didn't speak for a couple minutes.

"All jokin' aside," I finally said. "Do you think you can pull it off?" His answer surprised me.

"Will I ever see you again, Vit?" His eyes glimmered with tears. He blinked one free from his lids and it ran down his cheek and clung to his jaw. I inclined my head.

"Yeah, pard. You can visit me in the forest."

"Where ya gonna stay?"

"My lair."

"Where's that?"

I described it for him.

"You just gonna live there the rest of your life?" This question hit me like a kick in the gut. I was only thirteen years old. I had a full life ahead of me. Could I really spend it like the Daniel Boone of nineteenth century Tennessee? Even Boone had been captured by the Shawnee. And his son was killed by Indians. Did I have it in me to live the rest of my life in the wilderness?

"At least for a while. Then maybe I'll travel or something."

"I can handle it, Vit. The purtend death thing, I mean. I can pull it off."

"Thanks, pard. Can I sleep here tonight?"

"Course. I'll help you sneak out in the morning."

WE LAY SIDE BY SIDE IN HIS BED. THE MATTRESS SMELLED OF rot and mildew. The bedstraw was lumpy and uneven. I had grown so accustomed to my pine and cedar pallet in the lair, that it was hard to get comfortable. I was grateful though. It was nice to be on a mattress indoors for a change. Having some company was an extra benefit.

TWENTY-FIVE

The next morning we snuck out of the house before his pa stirred. Chester accompanied me to the tree line. He wished me luck. I thanked him for everything he was about to do. We shook hands and I took off into the trees. I kept to the forest parallel to the road on the south-facing slope of the hills that received more sunlight. I took my time picking my way through the woods, hopping from rock to rock and log to log where I could, and utilizing areas where the snow had melted to avoid leaving footprints. It wasn't long before I was in the bog where I had buried the bodies of the men I'd killed on the road.

After several minutes I found the burial site. The ground was still carpeted with snow, but I was able to use a familiar black willow tree as a reference. I kicked the piles of loose brush out of the way and scraped at the snow with my boot until I found the two mounds that contained the bodies. I stabbed at the earth with my staff. The mud was frozen hard and crunched loudly underneath.

It was clear I needed a shovel. No longer concerned about footprints, I plodded through the snow toward my farm. When the forest opened up before me, I paused to check if anyone was on the road. When I felt comfortable about it, I sprinted up the lane to the maple where my folks lay.

It was surreal seeing the ruins of my home and barn. The black of the charred timbers contrasted starkly with the gleaming snow. I listened to the wind whistle through the branches above me and thought of Ma and Pa and of my brother who lay somewhere alone in a battlefield under the dirt and snow.

The shovel still leaned against the maple, the head frozen to the ground. I kicked it free and threw it over my shoulder. I whispered goodbye to my folks and made it back to the bog.

I chose the body on the left because it was closer to my size. It was also the one I shot in the chest. I wanted an intact skull. Digging it up proved more difficult than I would have guessed. Chipping away at the mud was like breaking rock. By and by, I had uncovered a torso. The blue coat was still mostly intact, save for the bullet hole. The process of freeing the carcass from the grip of the frozen earth proved arduous and lengthy. My hands, ears, and nose burned from the cold and snot ran over my lips.

Yellow bone showed through the peeling skin on the carcass's face and hands. The eyes were frozen balls and covered with mud and ice. There was no discernible odor and the body was held together in a hunk of ice. Otherwise it would have pulled apart easily when I tugged it out of the trench.

When I was done refilling the hole and covering it with the brush, my fingers were bright red and numb. I breathed hot air on them and tucked them under my armpits until the feeling came back. I wiped my cheeks on my sleeve and covered my face with the sash and huddled on my haunches under the quilt until my body thawed enough to move again.

I tied one leg of Chester's trousers around the legs of the body and dragged it out of the bog to the edge of the field where I started the long haul to Dead Goat Hollow. The body was very heavy but the snow alleviated some of the friction. Stopping every few minutes to rest, it took me half an hour to get to my house. I sat on the head of the shovel to keep my butt dry and rubbed my hands.

Chester's trousers had torn during the haul, so after a few minutes of staring at what was left of my house, I set out to find a different solution. At the northern edge of our property along a small stream, I found a small copse of mimosa trees. The stalks were flexible and soft. I hacked down two stems that were as thick as my wrists and about eight feet long.

I dragged the poles back to the body where I stripped the bark into long straps. I wedged the poles under the corpse and secured it with the straps. I gripped the poles at the opposite end and lifted to test the integrity of the build. The corpse slid behind me on the makeshift sled as I walked a few steps. It seemed sturdy and operable.

With the shovel, my staff, and my belongings on top of the body, I lugged the sled toward the fields. It didn't escape my notice that last time I'd traveled this route, Thoreau dragged a similar sled behind him. Only instead of the corpse of a Yankee, he had been dragging Ma.

Halfway across the front field, I looked back at the house to bid it farewell again, and noticed the poles of my sled had cut tracks into the frosty mud. I dropped the sled and ran back to my starting point and scuffed up the ground with my boots and filled the gouges with soil and snow. For the rest of the journey, I'd repeat the process every hundred yards or so. Where I could, I ran the poles through the furrows in the field to reduce tracks.

Dusk had fallen when I reached Dead Goat Hollow. I scouted the area before I dragged the body to the camp. In the light of my candle, everything seemed as I had left it. The shelters were intact and there were no new footprints.

The only dry wood for miles around was the inside walls of the shelters. I felt sad doing it, but I had to use Thoreau's timberland barn as firewood. I built a large fire and lay the body beside it to thaw.

Wrapped in my quilt, I took great comfort sitting in the fire's heat. I couldn't help but stare at the corpse on the other side of the flickering flames. The situation I had found myself in was certainly unusual and my mind played with the impossibility of it as the wet wood in the fire hissed. After warming thoroughly, I searched the forest for more wood. I found a large tree that had fallen many years before. A section of it was propped a foot above the forest floor. The bottom side was still relatively dry and rotten.

I lay beside it and cut chunks free with my knife until I had a substantial pile. I carried an armful back to camp and put a big piece on the fire. The side of the body closest to the fire felt softer and more human. I rotated the carcass so the other side would get some heat, then followed the light of my candle back to the dead tree.

As I piled the wood in my arms, a deafening screech stabbed my ears from the darkness behind me. The witch.

Before I realized what I was doing, I had thrown the wood down, blown out the candle, and crawled under the tree. I had to cover my mouth with my hands to stifle my panting. My pulse drummed in my temples.

The forest was dark as ink and still. The witch had come back for me. Or had she come for the body? I didn't know what would be better for her stew, fresh or frozen human. I had no intention of finding out. The scream was a solitary one. No more followed. Only a light breeze through the dark branches and the hooting of an owl in the canopy twenty or thirty paces off filled the air.

After a number of minutes, I decided to investigate. As slowly as possible, I moved noiselessly from under the tree. Down the hill, the glow of the campfire blinked. It appeared the body was still there.

I felt around for my candle and stuffed it in my pocket, drew my knife and pistol, and took a careful step toward the fire. With every additional step, I felt the ground before me with my foot to make sure there wasn't any ice or twigs that would snap and alert the witch of my location. Keeping my eyes on the beacon of light, I made my way down at a snail's pace. Each measured step, I'd pause and listen to the forest before moving further.

It seemed an eternity before I felt the warmth of the fire again. There had been no signs of the witch and the body hadn't been disturbed. After some time, I calmed down enough to sit by the fire and stare at its hypnotic dance.

When I'd scanned the woods for intruders, I was completely blind. Anything beyond the immediate range of the firelight was obscured by bright, white circles in my eyes. I remembered reading about a trick pirates used to avoid light blindness. I tied the sash across my face diagonally to cover my right eye.

"This is kinda your fault, you know," I said to the body. The fire popped in response.

"If it weren't for you and your buddies, I might not be in this mess. If y'a'll had just minded your own consarn business, I could be at home with Ma, or with my friends at the McEwen house." I almost expected a response from the corpse, but it had nothing to say. Its frozen eyes stared at the dark canopy over my shoulder.

"But instead, I'm here in the cold forest talkin' to a dead body. And, if that ain't bad enough, there's a witch stalking me too." I listened to the crackling of the fire, my thoughts turning to tomorrow's plan and how everything might go down. Would everyone be convinced the body was mine? How long did I have to get everything ready? The conversation with Chester replayed in my mind. Then it dawned on me.

"Damnation!" I yelled out before I could catch myself. "I'm celebratin' New Year's Eve with the carcass of an Invader! Happy dad-blamed New Year's you bluebelly son of a sow!" My voice seemed confined to the camp, unable to penetrate the cold, heavy air. No echoes reported. For that I was grateful. Nevertheless, I felt vulnerable. I had announced my location to the witch, blubellies, or predators that might have been lurking about. Was Pa wrong? Did Indians scout this side of Backbone Ridge? Could there be a horde of savages creeping around just out of the firelight's reach?

I spun on my butt and stood facing the forest behind me. My left eye, filled with firelight informed me nothing about my surroundings. Pulling the sash down from my right eye and closing my left, I could make out dark gray columns of trees contrasting with a menacing black backdrop, a couple of twinkling stars, and my stretched and dysmorphic shadow gyrating in the yellow light dancing on the debris shelter. The only sounds were the crackling of the fire and a gentle babbling of the stream.

I sat down with my eye once again covered with the sash, looked over the flames with my exposed left and whispered, "I hate you and the rest of your filthy, invading comrades. I hope you're all drowning over and over in the River Styx."

I lay on my arm and drifted to sleep.

I AWOKE TO THE SOUND OF AN INSISTENT SQUIRREL chattering about the lousy weather or scolding its juveniles, and the stench of putrefying meat. It must have been a little before dawn. The forest, with the exception of the adamant squirrel, was quiet.

I had no way of knowing when Chester and the Vitus-is-dead-brigade would show up so I felt an overwhelming sense of urgency to move. The first order of business was to move the body into the shelter. I dragged it by the collar, the head, betrayed by the flaccid neck, dragged across the frost-ridden leaf litter. The pile of clothed flesh had thawed thoroughly and wanted to pull apart like tender rib meat at a pig roast.

I was able to keep it intact long enough to lay it down in the shelter. The next task would have been impossible if I had led an ordinary life up to this point. Using my knife, I cut the clothing off his body. The odor became a powerful force. It burned my nostrils. In many places, the gray skin, stuck to the fabric, peeled off with the cotton. Its left foot broke into two slabs of bone and flesh as I yanked the boot from it. The right foot nearly separated from the ankle.

I surmised my clothing to be rattier than Chester's, so I stripped down and slipped on his shirt and trousers as quickly as I could, the frigid air stabbing at my skin and raising gooseflesh. I rubbed my clothes in the mud near the fire where the heat had melted the frost. When they were sufficiently nasty, I tore bits and pieces away to match the rot patterns on the body's clothes. After choking and vomiting for the better part of a half hour dressing the corpse with my shirt and trousers, I meticulously replaced his boots.

The next problem to tackle was the face. It looked nothing like mine.

"You're a lot uglier than me," I said to the body. "Your hair could pass, but your jaw sticks out too much. Your teeth are too big. And that nose of yours is flat and wide."

The sharp cheekbones broke through the tight, flimsy skin like the blade of a shovel through the side of a feedbag. I plucked at a tag of the ruined flesh near the eye socket. It conceded its bone substrate easily, making me recoil in disgust, but affirming my idea. I reached out again and pulled at it again. Turning my eyes away, I peeled the skin off in a chunk about the size of a playing card. My eyes watered from the invasive odor that seemed to have worsened.

I carried the flap of skin to the stream and chucked it in, took a deep breath, and returned to my project. I removed the skin from the nose and shucked off the cartilage before knocking the front teeth out with a rock. I took another trip to the stream with the heinous cargo.

To the best of my ability, I had made the face unrecognizable. It could be construed as belonging to that of Vitus Swinggate or a random Yankee. Only Chester and I would know the difference.

I kicked leaves and debris over it to try and mimic what wind may have done over a period of weeks. Satisfied with my work, I lay the body's clothes on the coals until they caught fire and burned away any evidence the cadaver belonged to a Yankee. When it was gone, I scooped up handful after handful of water from the stream and doused the fire thoroughly. I threw the remaining buckles and buttons deep into the woods. Then I treated the ash pile with leaves and dirt to match the weathering of the body.

Sitting on a log, I studied the area, putting myself in the place of the authorities. Would this pass their scrutiny?

"What do you think, Chester," I said out loud to the impervious trees.

Intermittent clicking sounds started all around me in reply. The forest soon filled with the din of frozen rain smacking the leaf litter and tree branches. Little white balls bounced off the forest floor in front of me and battered my bare hands and ears.

This spurred me to get a move on. With some luck, the precipitation could help cover my tracks if I skedaddled promptly. I jumped up from the log and threw my cloak on, flipping the hood in place. A nearby beech tree, with branches that fanned into many reaching fingers, still clung to its brown, crispy leaves from the year before. The branch made an adequate broom for scratching up the areas in which I had walked and dragged the body. Once the forest floor could pass for undisturbed, I started up the hill.

After a few dozen paces, I looked back to be sure the camp looked copacetic. I hadn't left anything behind. My tracks weren't obvious. And the freezing raining, now mixing with snow, would soon cover the whole scene with a concealing blanket. For a moment, I played with the idea of staying to watch, but cold and hunger convinced me to move on.

Staring down at the camp where I "died," the sleet drummed all around me. A bird, perched a few trees away, sang as if it were saying "Go on! Go on!" With that I snapped out of my daze and started home to the lair.

TWENTY-SIX

The page margins of *Robinson Crusoe* were wide enough to serve as my field journal. I had already filled the title and opening pages with my recently-started memoirs. I felt it was important to capture my thoughts, accomplishments, failures, and disasters as I lived out the life of a fugitive. I spilled my guts on how I felt about my family's passing and the Yankees invading. It was both cathartic and time consuming.

A week or so after staging my death, I was writing on the top of page fifty-two about my most recent exploits when a soft crunching of forest debris drifted into the cave. I gently laid my book down and crawled slowly to the opening.

The crunching increased in frequency and volume. I grabbed the carbine, already loaded with a Minie ball, and trained it in the direction of the noise. I lowered to my stomach. The sights of the rifle bumped side to side with my panting.

From behind a large boulder, Chester's head emerged. I sighed as I lowered the rifle. He had no idea he had stumbled into the sight picture of a renowned sniper. His head swiveled, trying to locate the cave. I let out a short whistle. We made eye contact and his head nearly broke in two with a smile. He ran up the hill to me where we bear hugged and belly laughed.

"It seemed to take," he said as he investigated my home.

"Are you sure? Did they really think it was me? They're actually convinced I'm dead?"

"Yup, seems that way. Is that ratty old thing the book I gave you?" He pointed at *Robinson Crusoe* on the ground. It was twice its original size. The pages no longer laid flat and orderly. They were warped and yellowed from the elements and abuses of its owner. The worn leather cover strained to maintain the book's original shape. The swollen pages pulled the front and back covers ever further apart like a toothy smile.

"Yeah, that's it all right. How did everyone take it? Did anyone make a fuss?"

"I think they—"

"I mean," I interrupted, "did they really believe it? Was there a funeral? Did Addie cry and the whole thing?"

"They had a funeral for ya and everything."

"Really?"

He nodded.

"What happened at Dead Goat Hollow? Were you there? Did you go to the funeral?"

"Whoa, slow down, pard. I'll get to all of it."

"Well, go on, don't leave me hangin'.'"

"Yes, I was at the holler when they fount the body. I'm the one that led them there. The provost marshal, a couple Yankees, and the Colonel came. The Colonel seemed pretty well sure it was you and you was dead. At least that's what he was arguing."

"Arguing? Were they arguing?"

"Yeah, one of them Yankees didn't think it was you. I was gonna git to that in a minute."

"Was there a detective?"

"Not sure. Maybe the other Yankee that came. I don't know." He shrugged.

"Tell me about the funeral."

"Well, we buried you…I mean that man, next to yer Ma and Pa. There was me, and Addie. The Colonel and the missus. Two or three kids from the house. The Whittons and Mr. Carter. Mr. Whitton and Mr. Carter helped with the diggin'. When they was tired, me and Roger dug. It was a sad affair. The adults mostly just stayed quiet and shook their heads to and fro. Heck, I even cried a little."

"What about Addie? Was she sad?" I blurted out. I'd spent months speaking freely to figments of my imagination. Now that someone was actually around, I'd forgotten to filter my words.

"I mean, did she think it was real?" I said to save face. If he knew how awkward I felt, he didn't let on.

"Yeah, she was tore up, Vit. I'm not gonna lie. I had a hard time with it. She and I…"

He trailed off, shaking his head. I let him breathe.

"Listen, Vit," he started up again, "never mind that. I

gotta tell you 'bout that other man. The one that was arguin' with the Colonel."

"Sure," I said. "Go on."

"I think he's the brother of the man you killed."

My heart slammed against my breast bone.

"Which man I killed?" I asked between explosions in my chest. Before he answered, I knew what he was going to say.

"That Canfield fella. Zeke Canfield." My forehead filled with red heat.

"His brother, or whoever he is, ain't convinced yer dead. He's angry as a copperhead. Said he aims to keep lookin' for ya and ain't gonna stop till you're fount."

The world around me whirled. I couldn't catch my breath. Noticing the torment on my face, Chester said, "I can keep an eye out for ya. I'll alert you when he's comin' to this neck of the woods."

The effect of his words was instantaneous. My heart began to recover as if I had just slowed from a sprint. What he said made enough sense. There was no need to get bent out of shape yet.

A current of cold air poured over the roof of the cave sending chills through me before flowing farther down the ravine. Chester shivered too.

"Let's sit by the fire a spell," I said, hoping that concentrating on stoking the coals and rebuilding a fire would get my mind on something else.

We climbed into my lair and sat by the hearth where we sat with our outstretched hands roasting over the flames.

"You done some redecoratin'," he said. He smelled of

sweat. The scent of the McEwen house clung to his clothes. His bad breath clouded in front of him. Any smell foreign to my woodland surroundings and my own wild stench was distinct to me now.

"I don't want to spend our time together worryin' about that Canfield man," I said. "You just keep an eye on him for me if you will."

"Sure thing, pard. You know I will."

"Tell me about town. About the McEwen house. The other kids."

He told me stories about lessons with the McEwens, what the reverend said at church. Poked fun about his pa's shenanigans. He said he'd done some fishing, but it wasn't the same without his pard. It was nice hearing him talk about normal things. In his stories, there was no starving, no freezing half to death, crushing loneliness, dragging dead bodies through the forest, or burying parents. It was all normal kid stuff.

It was a nice distraction listening to his banter and living vicariously through him. The burning curiosity that neither of us addressed was that of Addie and whether or not she had feelings for me. But I guess, at the end of the day, it didn't matter. Nothing from the normal life mattered any more. I was dead. The finality of that thought fell on me like a hundred-year-old oak succumbing to a windstorm.

I wasn't gone on a trip. I hadn't moved to another town. I was gone forever. I could never go back and say, "Hi everyone, I'm home! Did you all miss me?" There would be no reunion with my playmates, my family. No one singing *For he's a jolly good fellow* upon my return. No claps on the back saying welcome back, Vitus.

There was no picking up where we left off. No starting over. I was forever the Fiend of the Forest, destined to live my life like a wild animal. A coyote wandering aimlessly, searching for food to drag back to a den, alluding humans while coveting their life from afar.

The sun started creeping behind the hill, pulling with it a dark blanket over the ravine. Chester stood and brushed his tail end off. "Well, pard. I guess I better get scootin'."

"Yeah," I said as I stood and stretched my legs. "Maybe you can come by every once in a while to visit and report the goings on with that Canfield fella. What does he look like, by the way?" I said. "I see hunters out here every now and again but I just let them pass. But if I knew what he looked like, I could catch him before he caught me."

"I don't really know. I couldn't get a good look at him. He's always got a big hat covering most of his face."

"See you before long?"

"Sure thing, pard."

"Maybe you could give me a whistle upon approach to let me know it's you comin'. That way I won't almost shoot your head off."

"I'd rather that." He extended his hand. I swatted it away and went in for a hug.

"Much obliged."

He blushed and nodded, then turned and crashed through the understory to the game trail. The cacophony of his foot falls, like a company of drunk soldiers, slowly faded and the woods fell quiet again. I spent an hour sweeping the forest floor with a branch from a beech tree to cover his tracks.

WINTER SEEMED TO HANG AROUND LIKE A HAIR IN A BISCUIT. I was low on food. I hadn't seen a rabbit in weeks, only an occasional squirrel in the tree tops. I was almost tempted to eat Grandpa, but couldn't bring myself to do it. He'd probably taste bitter anyway.

The idea of a nice turkey dinner overtook me suddenly and wouldn't release its grasp. From time to time, I had noticed a gathering of these delicious birds in a small clearing to the north of me. Because of Canfield, my rifle was not an option on account of its noise.

The answer to my obtaining turkey dinner silently dilemma came to me at a fallen Osage orange tree. The limbs of Osage were very strong and flexible. With my knife, I chopped one off that was relatively straight and about four feet long. I tied my boot lace to one end and leaning my weight on it to bend it, I tied the lace to the other end. The lace gave a nice twang as I strummed it. All I needed were some arrows. By and by, I found some cane shoots and crow feathers that, with a good deal of effort, I was able to fashion into serviceable arrows for my bow.

I practiced for a total of two hours and decided it was time to test my skills. It was close to sunset, when I spotted three turkeys in the clearing. I removed my boots, lay them in the ferns with my staff and crept softly toward the opening of the forest. Twenty yards from the closest bird, I figured I'd better not press my luck. I nocked my arrow, drew it back, steadied it, and released it. The arrow flew straight, but my aim was inadequate. It clipped the tail feathers, erupting all three turkeys into a gobbling, squawking fit. They half ran, half flew across the field into the forest.

I bolted after them but was unable to follow them for long. I sat on a log, dejected. What an idiot I was. I had blown the whole expedition because I didn't have the patience to train longer before engaging in such an endeavor. In desperation to devour a turkey leg, I acted rashly and ruined my chances of a feast.

The turkeys picked at the ground at the bottom of the ravine where two hills were separated by a creek. In winter the hills around Franklin looked like giant, golden-brown loaves of bread lined up, side by side on a baking pan. Only instead of a flakey crust, they were covered with winter-browned leaves and gray, empty trees.

A flash of crimson caught my eye as I stood to leave. When I moved closer, it became clear that it was a deer carcass under a beech sapling. It was carelessly covered with leaves and sticks. Around its body, patches of the floor showed rich soil with deep cuts in it as if someone had raked the forest debris onto the carcass to cover it up. I swept the hide off with my bow.

The chest cavity was ripped open, the heart, lungs, and liver gone. There were obvious gouges in the neck. The stomach had been removed, but the intestines remained neatly intact. Strangely enough, the hair around the open cavities almost appeared to have been shaved. Clumps of nipped hair lay around the body.

I leaned on my bow in contemplation. I had seen deer eaten by coyotes before, but the scene was usually a disorderly mess. Organs would be all over the place, and they usually chewed their way in through the back end. Never had I seen nipped hair.

This kill site was much neater than coyote, but not neat enough for a hunter. Additionally, no meat had been cut away. Someone or something must have been scared off before finishing its meal. It didn't appear to have been dead more than a day or two, so I took advantage of the great fortune I had stumbled upon. My failure and the failure of another predator had serendipitously provided me with something much greater than a lousy turkey dinner.

I pulled the intestines out and hefted the carcass over my shoulders, surprised by my growing strength. Grabbing my boots and staff on the way back, I carried my quarry to an outcropping on a hill about a quarter of a mile from the lair. I peeled the coat back and cut away the spoiled meat, leaving it for the coyotes. I carved off the back strap and tenderloin.

As I butchered the animal, I felt like someone was watching me. I surveyed the quiet forest, but saw no anomalies. Assured, there was no one around, I filled my basket with fresh, red meat. I had decided I'd come back for the hide and the rest of the meat the next morning. I marched, triumphantly back to the lair.

That night I roasted the back strap over a fire, and had a spiritual experience dining on charbroiled venison. The following morning, I returned to my deer cache and found it missing. Skid marks in the dirt suggested it had been dragged away.

"What on earth could have dragged that thing away?" I whispered to myself.

I carefully followed the drag marks, the shaking end of my staff leading the way, to an opening in a cliff face. My heart pounded in my temples. Inside a shallow cave, the deer remains lay half covered with dirt.

Like the day before, a heavy feeling of being watched pressed on me. I was momentarily paralyzed by its weight. I carefully scanned the forest and saw nothing out of the ordinary. "Was it the witch? Why would she move the deer? Is there another fiend in the forest? Coyotes? Why would coyotes try and bury it?" My mind stormed with questions. I made every effort to convince myself it was just coyotes behaving strangely.

Despite my fear the witch was staring at me from a cavity in a tree or the cave before me, I grabbed the hind leg of the deer and yanked it free from the dirt. At the bottom of the hill, with the entire ravine in view, I removed the hide and as much salvageable meat as I could.

Safely back in my little domicile, I cooked a venison dinner and scraped the deer skin. I hung the leftovers and hide above the fire to dry. My run at bow hunting was a flop, but by divine providence, or dumb luck, I came away from the failure with a new deerskin coat and weeks of jerky.

Winter seemed unusually long and bitter. The deerskin almost never left my back. Many days, I'd just wander the forest looking like half man, half deer, pole vaulting over ditches and creeks with my staff. If anyone clapped eyes on me, they'd surely run home to their family claiming they had seen some kind of savage beast, the likes of which had never been recorded in the biology books. When I thought about it, I'd smile a little because I was indeed like a monster in the woods Mary Shelley could have conjured.

I practiced my archery and slowly improved enough to kill a goose at a small pond. The leftovers of which, I shared with a new friend. A lone coyote had ventured close to camp to investigate the smell of roasted goose emanating from my home. He slinked close to the ground, sniffing upward. Several yards from me, I could see the battle in his eyes. Hunger, the more formidable force, was imposing its will on the coyote's innate coyness.

His ribs protruded from his fur like a xylophone. His quick breathing and twitchy face showed that hunger was winning out on wariness. By and by, he prostrated himself and took on a look of a beggar.

I rewarded his bravery with the neck and head, which I threw down the slope. After devouring the proffering without chewing, he inched closer a few more paces, guarded.

"You little rascal," I said to him. "I guess winter's been hard on you, too." My voice was rough and weak, hardly recognizable any longer.

"Well, come and get a little more."

Each time I'd fling undesirable goose parts at him to reinforce his daring, he'd get slightly closer.

For weeks after the goose dinner, he came and went every once in a while to beg for leftovers. Some days, I'd have a snack for him, but unfortunately, there were more days where I had nothing to offer.

"How's about you bring me something for once, you little rascal?" I asked him.

He was almost like a pet dog, only he never got closer than five or six yards of me and he'd never stick around long. Our relationship was clearly one-sided, but it was a relationship nonetheless. I named him Rascal and anticipated his return each day.

Winter slowly loosened its grasp and eventually bowed out and spring inched into place. It had been a while since I'd seen Rascal. Most nights I heard the eerie calls of his kind and hoped he was nearby. I made myself believe that he was the one watching me. Whose eyes I often felt upon me.

TWENTY-SEVEN

The forest was a thousand gray upward strokes from an artist's brush, branching and twisting. Weaving. Entwined and braided. All reaching for the sky in a never-ending competition for the sun's attention. The artist's brush dabbed spatters of green among the stretching branches. Canopies of shrubs had been completed, full of bright green clusters.

Blooming dogwoods were white splotches stabbing onto the canvas throughout the understory. Like snow reflecting light, the collection of petals brightened the otherwise brown and drab hillside.

Around me, purple trillium and toothwort stretched their new leaves as their young stems telescoped from the rich forest soil. Groups of mayapple, with umbrella-shaped leaves, cropped up like little villages.

Sipping dandelion coffee from my tin cup, the chirping of birds and chattering of squirrels suddenly stopped. The forest was quiet as a grave. A warning. Someone or something was approaching. Large wildlife often stalked the forest, but never had I witnessed the entire habitat going silent on account of it. Like a wild animal, my ears seemed to move forward on their own to gather more sound. My eyes bright and alert.

I was afraid to move on account of the noise I'd make. I figured if everything else was quiet and still, I should follow suit. A flash of color in the understory to my right caught my eye. For a fleeting moment, I thought a fox squirrel was walking on a low tree limb, but it became obvious that what I was seeing was a light brown cylinder of fur poking up from behind a mossy boulder, moving right to left. It made no sound.

I could tell right away it wasn't human, but the prospect of what it could be frightened me just as much. It stopped momentarily and poked its head out from behind the boulder. It didn't notice me at first. Its nose twitched and head turned toward me. We locked eyes. Its menacing, gold irises and dark pupils burned holes in me. Their squinting shape with the black lines around the lips made a permanent and intimidating scowl.

It had a white goatee with black edges. Its large ears, standing erect, rotated gently to pick up the slightest of sounds. Its intense eyes studied me like it'd never seen anything like me before. I was an unknown creature to it. I was crouched on a ledge above it as if ready to spring.

There was no fear or malice in its face. Just inquisition. It must have wondered what kind of creature I could be and whether I intended to do it harm. Could it tell I was also a predator because my eyes were wild and situated in the front of my head like a cat or a coyote? Was it deciding if I was dinner?

My face resembled a human, but was covered with grime. I put on my brave face and disallowed a discernible fear in my features. The hair on my head was long and wild and caked in mud and various forest debris. My torso and limbs were part black, brown, and green, like a monster. My back and sides were covered in dark hairs, a deer's winter coat. Moss grew in patches all over me and I reeked of mildew and mud.

No wild animal could be blamed for mistaking me for some anomalous creature. Since I had found the deer, I'd been enjoying its coat on frigid days, and my clothing had gone the way of the forest. The cotton of my clothing had rotted away in places and collected colonies of moss in others. Bathing in the winter months was few and far between. I'd occasionally wash my face in a trickling waterfall nearby and brush my teeth with pine needles. When they were blooming, I'd chew on wild mint to maintain my dental health. That was about the extent of my hygiene practices.

I had become part of the forest, just as a discarded mattress or neglected house would. Nature had moved in and given me a makeover. I looked and smelled like my environment.

After staring at me for an uncomfortable amount of time, the animal took a couple steps forward revealing its full body. It was a large, male cougar. He must have outweighed me by twofold.

With each measured step, muscles rippled under his tan coat through his legs and across his back. His feet absorbed each silent step with a thick padding on the bottoms. He was deadly, but beautiful in his form. Beautiful in his movement and behavior. Like me, it was a solitary animal that roamed the forest silently, stalking prey.

My heart hammered and my nerves sizzled. Was he going to determine I was prey, or would he just pass along? If he wanted to, he could cover the distance between us in a single bound, and he'd do it faster than I could grab a gun. If he wanted me, he had me.

If I ran, he'd surely chase me. Instead, I continued the staring contest with him. Addie had trained me for this with staring competitions. She was always the first to blink or smile. I firmly held my combat face. It seemed we were engaged for hours before the cat released me from its glare and quietly trotted off. The forest immediately returned to a din of chirping and chattering.

The distant sound of wind blowing from the fields grew in strength. Beyond the edge of the forest, yellow bunches of field turnips swayed in the breeze. Their roots would soon be good to eat. The wind rushed into the canopies of the trees and up the ravine, coursing through the tree tops like a giant, invisible serpent in search of prey.

The tree tops swayed above me and sang like a church congregation moving to music. The wind caressed my face, blowing my hair behind my ears. It was alive, a great spirit rushing over the earth or perhaps the breath of God. Invisible to the eye, but could cause destruction or make trees dance and gently stroke my face. I let out a boisterous sigh—relief the encounter with the large cat had been amicable and God or the Wind Spirit had watched over me.

The cougar reminded me how vigilant I had to remain. The forest in spring was a world apart from winter. I could move more freely among the bustling branches without fear of being heard. However, if my predators couldn't hear me, I couldn't hear them coming either.

The same could be said about visibility. The riot of new leaves in varying shades of green on tree branches and shrubs, and the blooming flowers vying for attention, all worked to reduce my field of vision. In many places, it was hard to see more than a few yards. I was concealed by my surroundings, but so too were my enemies.

The song of a spring peeper carried up the ravine bottom and pulled me out of my dream world. It was a warm spring morning. My stomach grumbled as I stood to stretch. I stirred up the coals from last night's fire and warmed water for my coffee.

The scent of violets drew me down the slope to a patch of sun where their candied petals glistened with dew. I collected a handful of purple velvet and tossed it in my mouth. The arrival of spring had never been so sweet.

A bluejay hollered and a few crows flew off. A crunching, heavy and measured, replaced the caws of the black birds. Shuffling from one direction back to another as if foraging. I quickly hopped on to a fallen tulip poplar that stretched, long and straight over a large expanse above a ditch. I snuck across the smooth bridge, well-worn from my travels over it, and perched on a boulder, listening. The crunching continued in its erratic pattern.

The newly emerging leaves obscured my view. The

Canfield man would have dogs or horses, maybe friends with him. His movements would have been more like a hunter. Whatever was moving was not making any attempt at being stealthy. I stayed wary.

By and by, there was a voice. "Vitus." Then a whistle.

"What are you doing, you knucklehead?" I yelled out to the trees. "Chester, get up here before I put a bullet in you."

"Whoa, pard. It's just the Easter Bunny!"

"The what?" I said to myself.

A leafy sapling moved, from behind it emerged Chester with a basket. "Happy Easter, Vit!"

"What are you up to?" I said.

"I didn't even see you sittin' there. You kinda look like a tree stump or something."

As he closed within a couple yards, his face contorted. "Vit, you look like a wild animal, and buddy, you smell like one too."

We shook hands.

"Did you come to just pick on me?" I asked.

"No. I'm the Easter Bunny and I brought you some Easter eggs. But you have to find them."

"Oh, real funny. You're gonna make me forage? That's a good one."

"Come on, be a good sport. We used to love egg hunts at the McEwens' when we was kids."

"You know all I do is search for food, right?" A little grin stretched my cheeks despite myself.

"Come on, they're not that hard to find."

"Oh, all right," I groaned as I stood on stiff legs. He

was holding out the empty basket for me, hopping up and down with an open smile. It made me almost giddy.

"Give me the darn thing," I said as I ripped it from him and took off into the brush. He followed to supervise. It was only a few minutes of running, slipping on rotten leaves, and laughing before I had found four eggs.

"That's all of 'em," he said. "Sorry I couldn't get more."

I threw my arm over his shoulders. "That's quite all right, pard. Much obliged."

We sat by the coals of my fire to take inventory. There were two brown and two white hardboiled eggs.

"Go on, bust one open."

He refused one I proffered. He smiled as he watched me eat. It was the most delicious thing I'd put in my mouth since the goose a few weeks back. It felt filling and satisfying. I nearly teared up.

"Thanks, Chester. Yer a good friend you know that?"

"Well, I guess I better be on my way," he said.

"Thanks again, pard."

He stopped after a few paces down the hill and turned. "I almost forgot." He palmed his head as if to punish himself for his absentmindedness. "One of my sources says the Canfield man's scarin' up some hounds."

"Yeah, that's probably worth knowing, Chester. Geez, I'm glad you remembered before you left."

"Sorry, pard. I was just so happy to be your Easter rabbit."

"What's his plan, do you know? And what's this about 'your sources'?"

"I think it's gonna be a few weeks, but once he has a pack, he's gonna be comin' for ya. I'll keep an eye out for ya. But so far, he's been lookin' mostly to the south of town. I think yer all right for now."

I let out a deep breath. "I don't know what I'd do without you, pard."

"Have you come up with a plan yet?"

"How's that?"

"I mean, are you gonna just live in this cave the rest of yer life?"

"What do you propose I do? I ain't got a family. I only have one friend. I'm dead to everyone else. I ain't got a purpose no more, Chester." His question had struck a chord that must have been hiding under the surface. It came out of nowhere and was unbridled by proper grammar.

"Oh, my. I'm sorry, Vit. I didn't mean to make you sore. I just wondered if you knew what you were gonna do."

"Sorry. I didn't mean to jump down yer throat. You're all I got." A few seconds of silence passed.

"Well, whatever you do," he started back up. "Make sure you let me know, okay?"

"Okay."

"If you aim to run off for good, I'm comin' with ya. You understand?"

"Yeah."

"Honor bright, Vit?"

"Honor bright."

He turned back down the hill and disappeared into the woods, heading back to the world I'd never know again.

TWENTY-EIGHT

Returning from my traps empty-handed, I had a tremendous fright. Bounding over roots and rocks, I came to a sudden halt when an anomaly glared like a train light from the soil below.

A boot print. Then another. And they were heading toward the lair. An intense fear gripped me, bringing to mind the unforgettable moment when Robinson Crusoe found a human foot print on the beach of his island. "Had I walked on this path and forgotten?" I asked myself. "Could I have been so careless?" I looked at my feet, my dirty toes wiggled at me. On account of the mild weather, I had been barefoot for going on a week now.

The prints before me were fresh. The edges of them were sharp and clear. If I had lost my mind and walked this trail a week or more ago in my boots, the edges would be rounded and less distinct.

Stunned, I stared and studied the prints. There was only one set. "Only one person," I whispered to myself and imaginary Chester and Addie behind me. "Are they adult size?" I said to myself.

"Are they mine?" imaginary Chester asked.

"Are they Chester's?"

I set my foot inside the track. The outline was too small to fit my foot. Relieved that whoever it was had a smaller foot than my own, I snuck forward. If it wasn't Chester, I was prepared to use my staff for the first time on a human foe.

I stayed low and used my pattern of silent movement to close in on the lair.

"Vitus. There you are!"

I started at the sound of his voice and nearly lost my footing on the hill.

"Consarn, Chester! You gave me a real fright!" I climbed the slope. He paced back and forth in front of the mouth of the cave, wringing his hands.

"Vitus, we gotta go."

"Slow down! What's the matter?"

"I think they're comin' soon, pard."

I touched his arm. "How do you know?"

"They're mappin' out the search area. I seen it. They got blood hounds and mean old mongrels too. They got horses and guns."

"That's some good reconnaissance work," I said to set him at ease a bit.

"You hear what I said, Vit? Guns! Dogs! Horses! Yer done for. Let's get out of here now. Come on, let's go!"

"When are they coming?" I tried to keep a calm tone.

"Not sure, but they's talkin' bout comin' this way soon."

"Let's calm down a second, pard. What makes you so sure?"

"Vit, I've been doing espionage for you like we said. This Canfield man been meetin' with a couple other fellas a lot lately outside behind Whitton's. They don't make no mind of me on account of my being a kid and all. I saw them lookin' at the map and pointin' this direction while they done so."

"When was that?' I butted in.

"Yesterday."

I laid my hand on his shoulder. "Well they probably won't get over this way for a day or two. Besides, their horses can't travel through the forest in these parts." My words had a calming effect on him. I almost reassured myself in the process.

"There's more, Vit."

"What?"

"There's been talk about the Yankees inscriptin' young kids like us—boys with parents who don't give a hoot 'bout their kids."

"Inscriptin'?" I said. "You mean conscripting?"

"Yeah, whatever."

"What do you mean?"

"Me and some of the other boys that come to the McEwen house, like Roger and Sam, might get takin' away in the bluebelly army."

"Surely you jest," I said.

"I jest not."

"And the Colonel is just going to let it happen?" I asked.

"Nothin' he can do 'bout it, I guess. We ain't his kin."

"And your pa?"

"He put up a weak fight, but in the end, he didn't really give a rat's bald tail. The Yanks promised to give him a small payment for my service. And that's the extent of the convincin'. Then Pa said on account of my age, it didn't matter which side I fought on. He said I'd just be an errand boy or a drummer. I don't know how to play the drum, Vit. I especially don't know no Yankee songs."

We were both silent for a moment. I was trying to take it all in. Chester's pa was such a low life. He'd do anything to get his hands on more bug juice.

"Let's just go," Chester broke the silence. "The two of us. We'll skedaddle and never come back."

"Yeah, I like the sound of that," I said.

I did like the idea of my pard and me running off. It was my chance to protect Chester. To keep him safe from his pa and the Invaders. He'd done more than his share to take care of me. And it was time to admit to myself that I was in over my head now. What could I do against a legion of Yankee vigilantes and their dogs?

"We still have a little time. We need provisions before we go. Can you get some food and anything else we could need from the McEwens?"

He nodded.

"We can meet at your house at sundown and be on our way."

"I can't tonight," he said. "Pa said he'll take me fishin' this evening, and I really want to go. Me and him ain't gone fishin' in a coon's age. How 'bout sundown tomorrow?"

"Do you have to go with your pa?"

"He'll get suspicious if I don't show up."

"I guess that'll work."

"Okay, so meet me at my house tomorrow at dusk, right?"

"Right. When I get there, I'll hide in the western edge of your forest until dusk."

He bear hugged me before sliding down the hill.

I WAS BESIDE MYSELF. I FELT STRANGELY REVIVED AT THE prospect of an adventure. I had purpose again. Even if that purpose was to evade a ruthless hunter. And having Chester along made it all the more invigorating.

Nervous energy ruined any chance I had of sleeping that night. The prospect of leaving the lair and leaving Franklin forever strangely weighed on me. The thought of never seeing Addie again after tomorrow twisted my gut into tight coils. I wouldn't even be able to view her from afar. "Maybe I can go say goodbye to her anyway," I said quietly aloud. "No, stupid," I returned. "I'm dead to her."

As the skies turned gray, the idea of seeing Addie had not faded. It had only grown in strength, worming itself deep into my brain, settling in with no plans of leaving. Despite my efforts to shake the thought free, I was under a vicious, withering attack.

I threw a barrage of counter offensives at my mental adversary. I tried to visualize future adventures with Chester. On the opposite end of my imaginings, I saw myself hanging from a noose over the courthouse steps. I fought valiantly, but the vision of Addie proved to be a formidable opponent. Eventually, emotional casualties mounted and I had to find a distraction.

I decided to tidy up the lair and take inventory of items I would leave behind, and supplies I'd take with me. That done, I alternated between my favorite chapters of *Daniel Boone* and *Robinson Crusoe,* interrupting their narratives with invasive thoughts.

"I'll just watch the McEwen house for a few minutes from the forest," I said to myself. "If she happened to pass by a window, I'd get to see her. I'll only wait one hour."

"One hour?" I questioned myself. "I thought it was only a few minutes."

"What's it going to hurt?" I asked the empty cave.

It was settled. I was going to see Addie one more time before I left.

I considered my plan thoroughly. I hadn't been to town in a very long time. If I was going to do this, I'd have to be very careful.

I dressed in my night clothes that I had fashioned from Ma's funeral cloak. My face was covered with a black mask of lace. I painted my bare hands and the skin around my eyes with charcoal. I tucked my knife and field glasses in my belt, sprinkled dirt on the coals of the fire, spun the staff, and bounded over the rocks to the top of the hill.

The light had faded before I reached town. I didn't get as close to the McEwen house as I'd hoped on account of there being people on the road. I climbed a black walnut tree and settled into the elbow of the highest limbs I could.

The McEwen house was mostly dark. One room downstairs was lit by a lamp. The golden rectangle of the window wheeled around in my sight picture. Eventually, I zeroed it in and brought it to focus. I could discern no movement inside, but could make out vague shapes of a table and sofa. Seeing the interior of that house pulled strongly at my heart.

I waited for the better part of an hour before an upstairs window began to glow. The image bobbed up and down in my glasses in response to my increase in blood pressure. Finally settling, I was able to make out a figure for the briefest of moments. Judging by the size, I'd have to guess it was Mrs. McEwen. The figure closed the curtains, subduing the light and thus ending my peeping.

I climbed down the tree and made quick passage back to my refuge in the forest.

IN THE MORNING, I CHECKED MY TRAPS TO SEE IF THE FOREST was going to give me a farewell meal. It didn't. I activated each one so they wouldn't catch critters unnecessarily. Back at the lair, I laid out my pistol, staff, and knife. I decided to travel light. The rest of my belongings would have to stay behind.

The back of the cave funneled into a shaft, just wide and long enough to squeeze the length of my body into. At the end of the tunnel, was a small, dry chamber I'd been using for storage. I wrapped the rifles and Excalibur in a quilt and wrapped my books in Ma's funeral cloak. I neatly stowed the bundle in the chamber along with pots and other small belongings. I gently placed my chess pieces in one of the pots before I covered the entrance to the storage chamber with a large slab of limestone.

I removed my pallet and pulled down the wall of cedar

branches and scattered them throughout the surrounding forest. After covering the ashes of my campfire with dirt, I stood outside the opening and observed my work. My lair had been restored to its original state. I had left no evidence the Fiend of the Forest had once inhabited the cave. "Goodbye lair, you've been good to me. Goodbye Grandpa. Take care little friend."

Fighting back tears, I hopped from root to root and rock to log until reaching the game trail that had served as my personal sidewalk for so many months. I headed west.

I stopped for a snack at a patch of early blackberries and pocketed a handful for Chester. The tiny seeds cracked between my teeth and I sighed audibly at the tart flavor. I threw another berry in my mouth.

At full chisel, I sprinted giddily through fields and woods until I neared Chester's house. I was early. Dusk was at least an hour away.

I squatted under a bush at the forest margin and watched for Chester. There was no perceptible movement from his house. Daylight faded to gray and still no sign of Chester. There was no sign of life inside the house when I peered in his window. I gently tapped on the glass. Nothing.

I spun on my heel at the sound of a footfall behind me. I was suddenly staring down the barrel of a rifle. At the other end was the smirk of Chester's pa.

He spit a quid at my feet. "Hello, two hundred dollars."

I took a step back.

"I will shoot ya boy, if you don't do as yer told," he said

jabbing the barrel at me. "We're going to town, you and me."

"Where's Chester?" I asked, trying to stay calm.

"Probably half way to Atlanta by now." More tobacco squirted from his mouth. A stream of it wormed down his chin and fell on his shirt. He was so disgusting.

"Put your hands in the air, boy."

I did as he said and raised my hands above my head. I mentally rehearsed how I was going to grab the barrel with my left hand and punch him with my right. When he took a step closer, I knew I had him. But then he stopped, eyeing me suspiciously.

"Turn around," he said.

I turned and looked into Chester's window. The house was still dark and depressing. He'd been sold down the line by his own father and would probably never occupy that room again.

An image reflected off the glass. The butt of the rifle raised from behind my head. Before everything went dark, I realized that after all the months I'd spent getting away with murder, espionage, and thievery, and surviving on my own in the wilderness, I was being outsmarted by a no good drunk.

TWENTY-NINE

It was hard to decipher the dream world from reality when the effects of the blow to my head wore off. When I opened my eyes, the world around me was darker. I couldn't see my hand in front of my face. The floor beneath me was muddy. The air was musty. I was leaning against a large rock. Was I back in the lair?

The last thing I remembered was the sickening thud of the rifle butt slamming into the back of my head. It didn't make sense for me to be in my cave. In a state of confusion, I felt around. My head throbbed. The large stone I had been leaning against was smooth and straight. It met with another similar stone, making a ninety degree angle. A corner. I followed more stones to a second corner. I was in a room, not my lair.

The third corner wasn't there. What I found instead was a row of iron bars. Very solid iron bars. Overwhelming grief and disappointment cascaded through my body as I collapsed face first into the mud.

I wallowed in the cell for what felt like days. The darkness remained complete and unchanging. It was impossible to tell night from day. No one was about. No neighboring cellmates. No guards. No visitors. Just me and my thoughts. Thoughts that became increasingly despondent, inching toward lunacy. My grip on sanity weakened with each passing hour.

A torrent of freezing water hit my face.

"Wake up boy!"

There were dark figures outside my cell silhouetted by a torch at the end of the passage.

"Look at em, boys! It's the Fiend of the Forest!" a deep voice called out, rattling my bones.

"He doesn't look so tough to me."

"He's just a kid."

"A nasty little thing."

I could feel more then see their faces at the bars.

"Captain Canfield's gonna be real happy to see this horse turd!"

Another bucketful of water crashed over my body. I curled up and shivered violently. Their voices and the torchlight trailed off leaving me in the dark silence again. I lay in the mud thinking of Pa. Had he been in this same cell? Did he spend his last days in this pit of despair?

A METAL CLANK AND GRINDING YANKED ME FROM MY SLEEP. Men's voices bounced back and forth between the stone walls. A dim glow grew in what I could then see was a corridor. This was it, I thought to myself. They've come to hang me.

The light of the lantern intensified until it nearly blinded my fragile eyes. It stopped in front of my cell.

"Vitus." The voice was familiar. "I don't even recognize you."

I rubbed my eyes and gave them a minute to adjust to the light. The face became clearer. It floated in the golden light of the lantern, like an angel had come to visit me. To take me to my eternal home. Perhaps then, I had died and St. Peter himself was here to discuss whether I'd see my family in heaven or if I'd rot in hell.

"You're in a world of trouble, son," he said. "And I'm afraid there isn't much I can do about it."

"So I'm going to hell, then?" My voice was weak.

"Yes, you're going to hell for what you did," said another voice in the dark passageway.

It didn't sound like something St. Peter would say.

The Colonel's face was soft and caring. His eyes were dark pools with golden flecks of light glistening on the surface. He looked older and in some way, he looked frail. There was a seriousness in his features that revealed the gravity of the situation.

He turned his head toward the other voice. "Can you give us a minute?"

Footfalls faded into the abyss. The Colonel's golden face pressed through the bars.

"I can't say for sure where you'll end up, son. But you're not long for this earth."

"I'm to be hung like Pa?" I burst out as I crawled toward the light.

I fell against the bars and wept like a child. The shame

of seeing the Colonel and hearing my death sentence from him splintered my soul.

"Why are you here?" I said through sobs.

"Vitus, I'm afraid it's not as easy as a hanging." There was great sympathy in his voice.

I whimpered in the elbow of my sleeve. He reached through and patted my head.

"What do you mean, Colonel?"

"The men holding you here are determined to make a spectacle of you. Zeke Canfield is making his way back from the south. And when he arrives in the morning, they intend to put on a good show on your account."

My mind struggled to comprehend what he said. Zeke Canfield was in hell for sure. I had never heard the Colonel refer to hell as the south. Was the man with the birthmark returning from the dead to exact revenge?

The Colonel interrupted my thoughts.

"Canfield was leading a small contingent toward Atlanta, but they sent word of your capture and promised to delay your execution until he came back."

"Sir, I don't understand what you're talking about."

"A lot has changed since you disappeared. Canfield was promoted from guard duty at our house to sergeant. Anyway, long story short, he conscripted several of the boys and headed south."

Eddies of confusion swirled in my head.

"Son, Chester's gone."

He went silent. Drops of water echoed in the darkness behind him. The flames of the torch flapped like a flag.

I sat up straighter and inched closer.

"He took Chester, Vitus. Roger and Sam too. He left

Jimmy McKlusky on account of you beating him silly. Funny how things work out—"

"Sir!" My patience had grown thin and my temper to a fever pitch. I was almost ashamed of myself for yelling out. I took a breath during his stunned silence.

"Colonel, you said Zeke Canfield took Chester south. Zeke Canfield is dead and in hell. I killed him myself. How could he have taken the boys to hell with him?"

The Colonel sat against the corridor wall.

"I didn't realize how little you knew." He wedged the torch between two stones and unbuttoned his jacket. His movement was stiff, as if he was nursing a hurt rib. He sat on the wet stones and adjusted his trousers so he could cross his legs.

"Vitus, you didn't kill Zeke Canfield."

A goose egg grew in my throat.

"You killed his twin brother, Bill Canfield."

I suddenly became lightheaded and succumbed to the deluge of emotions. Everything went dark.

"Vitus, are you okay?"

I responded with a little grunt as I regained consciousness. I stewed momentarily in my anger and bewilderment, while the Colonel let me get my mental bearings. Sensing my torment, he spelled it out for me in plain language.

"Vitus, the man you meant to kill is alive and well. His brother was nearly identical. It was an easy mistake. Truth be told, I wish you had killed the correct brother, because Zeke was a deviant. He was uncouth. I didn't much care for the way he looked at Mrs. McEwen or how he treated

Adelicia and her sisters. And I learned from Chester what he had done to your house.

"And now he's heading to Georgia with your best friend to fight with the Yankees. So, I get it. He's a snake. I understand why you did what you did—or thought you did—but, to be clear, I do not condone any of it. You have definitely committed many grievous sins. You deserve to be executed for his murder and the murder of all the other men whose lives you took."

"Colonel. Why are you here? If you think I deserve to die, why are you here?"

"You killed Zeke Canfield's brother and he wants revenge. They're going to torture you in the most heinous ways until you die. God knows what kind of humiliation they'll submit you to in front of the townspeople."

His words hung in the air for a moment as I soaked it all in. I felt like I was in a dream. A nightmare.

"I'm here in an effort to convince them to hang you properly. I hate what you have become, Vitus, but you are indeed a murderer. I also understand we are at war and the lives you took were those of the occupying force. Your murders, though dishonorable, could be categorized as soldierly acts. As such, I feel you should be tried by the court and if found guilty, hung in proper fashion. You are owed due process. Unfortunately, I have failed to convince them to turn you over to the court."

"So, you're going to let them rip me limb from limb?"

"You are like a son to me and you're very important to my Addie. Because of that, I felt obligated to defend you from the Yankees' idea of retribution. I am afraid my efforts were fruitless. Canfield is hurrying back as we speak. I'm sorry, Vitus."

We sat in silence for several minutes.

"There's nothing more I can do, son."

I crossed my arms on top of my knees and buried my eyes in the sleeves and cried.

"I have to go now, Vitus."

His image wavered through my tears.

"I brought this for you." He pulled a small loaf of bread from his jacket pocket.

"It's Mammy's famous gingerbread. She made this one special for you this morning."

"Colonel."

"Yes, son."

"I'm sorry. I'm sorry for letting you down. I'm sorry for becoming a monster. I'm mostly sorry that I disappointed Addie." More tears coursed over my cheeks.

"I wish things would have worked out differently for you, Vitus." He handed the bread through the bars. I accepted it.

"Make peace with the Lord, Vitus."

"Colonel, could you tell Addie I'm sorry and that I'll miss her? Tell her goodbye?"

"Yes, son. I will."

He picked up the torch and made as if to leave.

"Colonel. Please don't let Addie watch. Make her stay home tomorrow. It's my final request. I can't bear the thought of her seeing me like this."

"I can do that for you, son."

He started down the corridor. Before he turned the corner, the torchlight paused and his neck twisted back toward me, "Don't eat the bread too fast. It'll make you sick if you do."

He disappeared into the inky black. The Colonel was gone.

The bread smelled heavenly. It reminded me of all the mornings I had spent at the McEwen House with all the other boys, learning our math and grammar. Addie and her sisters were always nearby. Mammy usually cooking something up or doing the laundry. The Colonel's library, and our secret conferences.

The fresh, ginger scent bathed my nose. It somehow smelled of hope. A fragment of joy in the otherwise hellish situation in which I had found myself. I gripped my last meal in both hands and broke it in half, only the halves didn't break away easily, as if something held them together. Something stiff.

I separated the two pieces and carefully investigated the soft bread in the dark. Nestled inside the soft core was something hard, recognizable to the touch. The Colonel's small folding knife. Caressing it in my hands, I wiped dough from the bone handle and flipped out the steel blade. The caked mud on my face cracked as my lips curled upward.

Thank you for reading. If you'd like to read Vitus's next adventure, grab War Path today!

Made in United States
Orlando, FL
29 September 2024